THE CRONE WARS

2

A GATHERING OF CRONES

LYDIA M. HAWKE

Published by Michem Publishing,
Canada

A GATHERING OF CRONES
January 2022
Copyright © 2022 by Linda Poitevin

Cover design by Deranged Doctor Design
Interior design by authorTree

ISBN: 978-1-989457-09-2
MICHEM PUBLISHING

CHAPTER 1

THE CROWS WERE BACK.

Three times they circled the clock tower before settling onto the roof of the Village of Confluence's hundred-year-old limestone town hall. An entire murder of them. Silent. Waiting. Watching me from across the sweep of treed lawn and the wide main street where I stared out the window of the Java Hut coffee shop.

"Are you even listening to me?" My son Paul's voice cut across the background chatter of the other patrons, his tone impatient. Peevish.

Much like his father's had been all the years we'd been married. The thought slipped into my mind before I could guard against it. Similar thoughts had been surfacing regularly, ever since...well. No need to dwell.

I sat up straighter on my stool—why couldn't coffee shops provide decent seating anymore?—and turned my attention back to Paul. But not my full attention, because I'd learned from experience that silent, watching, waiting crows did not bode well, especially if these were the kind I thought they were.

My gaze strayed briefly to a tall, bearded man lounging against the streetlight outside the window. If you didn't know him, everything about his demeanor would seem casual—from the fingertips tucked into pockets to the easy slouch of his powerful shoulders.

If you didn't know him.

I did.

I knew that he could shift like smoke from a human into a wolf, leaving his empty clothes in a pile at his feet. That he could transition back just as fast. That he would be naked when he did, and that the man-bun he wore would not survive the

1

change. I knew that he would die to protect me, and that nothing had moved on the street—in any direction—that he hadn't noticed, wasn't tracking. Except he hadn't once glanced at the town hall's roof, which meant I was right. These were the kind of crows only I could see. My own personal harbingers.

Which meant someone—or something—was coming. The goliath again? Icy prickles crept over my skin at the thought of the monster that plagued my nightmares. Paul growled under his breath, and I wrenched my gaze back to him.

"Sorry," I said. "I got distracted. You were saying?"

Something about how concerned he was about my well-being, I suspected. Again. It had become a familiar and unaltering conversation every time we'd spoken in the six weeks since the ... incident. My brain shied from the memories, the loss of control, the devastation I'd wreaked.

The casualties.

Paul frowned. Peevish he might be, but the concern in his brown eyes was genuine. "Honestly, Mom, I'm getting really worried about you. Ever since Edie—your house—you just haven't been the same."

I held back a snort. Goddess, he had no idea. I injected a reassurance into my voice that I decidedly did not feel. "I keep telling you I'm fine, Paul, and I am. I promise."

"Liar," an inner voice accused. It was the one I'd come to think of as my Claire-voice, one of three that lived in my head—voices, not Claires, because oh, goddess, I didn't think I could live with three of those. A second voice belonged to my departed best friend, Edith James, better known—or formerly so—as Edie; and the third was a mysterious voice I hadn't heard since it had urged me to summon water in my battle with the fire pixies. I'd briefly considered the possibility that one might be the Morrigan, but it sounded nothing like her harsh rasp—assuming that really *had* been the goddess I'd met that night, and not just a fever-induced hallucination after the gnome bit me.

I wondered what my already-worried son would think of the

voices, especially if he knew how the Claire and Edie ones were constantly at odds with—

"*Mom.*"

Shit.

"Yes." I sat up straighter and tightened my clutch on the cup of cold coffee before me, using it to anchor myself to the present. The here and now. A few tables away, a group of women laughed uproariously at something. I used that as an anchor, too. "Yes. I'm listening."

My son scowled. "But you're *not*," he snapped. "We've been having this same conversation for weeks now, and you haven't heard a thing I've said. I'm *worried* about you, damn it. You refuse to tell me where you're living, except that it's with that Lucan character"—he jerked his head toward the man on the sidewalk outside—"you never come to visit us anymore, you're avoiding your friends—you didn't even go to Edie's funeral, for God's sake. You're not just distracted, Mom, you're freaking evasive. This isn't *you*."

I sighed. I supposed that from his perspective, he had a point. But from mine, the person I'd been before seemed more foreign to me than the one I was now—even when I factored in my insecurities and flat-out terror at what lay before me.

Paul reached across the polished wood table and put a gentle hand over my wrist. "Listen, I talked with Dad, and we think—"

"Excuse me?" I pulled away, crows and voices forgotten. "You *what*?"

Brick red crept up Paul's neck to stain his cheeks. "He's not the enemy you think he is, Mom. He still cares about you."

"Right. Which is why he's a living cliché, married to his assistant and starting a new family at his age." I waved away my own words even as the sound of them died away, not wanting them to be misunderstood. "And I'm not saying that because I want him back, believe me. I've more than moved on."

"Given you're living with a man half your age, it would be hard *not* to believe you."

3

I ignored the snipe. "The point is, your father is no longer part of my life, and you have no business discussing me with him. At all. For any reason. Ever."

A part of me would have liked to know how the conversation had gone between Paul and my ex-husband—specifically, what Jeff had said—but a greater part of me was smart enough not to ask, because I really had moved on from that part of my life. How could I not, after my entire world had been turned inside out and upside down?

I glanced out the window at the town hall roof and the crows still perched there. The prickles along my skin returned. Something was coming, but what?

"Except Dad knows you better than anyone," Paul said, "and—"

I gave a sharp bark of laughter. "You're kidding, right?"

He leaned back in his chair, running impatient fingers through his hair. "Christ, Mom, how can I get through to you? I don't know what to do with you anymore."

Do with me? What was I, a slab of meat? I held onto my patience with both hands and attempted not to glower at my son. "You could try having a cup of coffee and a simple conversation with me," I said, my voice tart despite my best efforts. "Maybe tell me how Natalie and Braden are doing? How work is going?"

I regretted the words as soon as they left my lips. *Wrong direction, Claire. Definitely the wrong direction.*

"And maybe I wouldn't have to tell you if you'd come see them for yourself." Paul leaned forward again, elbows on the table and shoulders hunched. "Don't you get it, Mom? *That's* why I'm worried. You used to come by two or three times a week at least, if not more, and now we get nothing but excuses from you. We haven't seen you since your house burned down and Edie—" He broke off, visibly regrouped, and tried again. "Braden misses you. *I* miss you. Hell, I'm lucky if I get a call

4

from you once a week, and it was like moving a mountain just to get you to meet me today."

Because it's safer that way. I slanted a glance at the crows and the wolf-shifter waiting for me. Willing to die for me. *Because you have seen me since then, but you don't remember. Because I almost lost all of you, and now something else is coming, and I don't know enough yet to keep you safe. I might never know enough to keep you safe. Not from the Mages. Not from a god.*

Not from me.

"For God's sake, Mom, *talk* to me. Tell me what the hell is going on." The peevishness had returned to Paul's voice, but it was underlined by worry. Love. Pain.

My heart squeezed in on itself, and it was my turn to place a hand over his. "I'm sorry, but I really don't know what to tell you, Paul. You can see for yourself that I'm fine. Lucan and Keven take good care of—"

"Keven?" Paul gaped at me. "Who in God's name is Keven? You're living with *two* men? What the actual hell, Mom?"

Despite the startled glances directed our way from the other patrons, I almost laughed at the questions tumbling from him—and the utter shock on his face.

For a brief moment, I wished I could tell him everything, but it would have just made matters worse. Goddess, if he thought his quiet, mild-mannered, sixty-year-old mother taking up with two men was surprising, what would he do with the truth? The knowledge that Keven was a walking, talking, living gargoyle from Camelot itself. That Lucan was a Knight of the Round Table turned wolf-shifter by Merlin, who'd been possessed by Morok, god of darkness and deceit. That Merlin-Morok was here, now, in this lifetime, trying to open a portal back to that final battle of Camlann, where half his powers remained because the goddess Morrigan had caused them to splinter, trapped in a piece of the world itself. That over the centuries since, the Morrigan's magick had been wielded by four Crones who had

5

continued to split Morok's powers—and the world—again and again, creating the multiverse theorized but unproven by science. That another split might destroy the planet and all on it.

That I'd discovered six weeks ago that I was the Fifth Crone, tasked with separating Morok from his stolen mortal body and sending him back to the god-world, and the crows were back, and now—now something was coming, and honestly? The idea of me living with two men, even if it were true, was the least of Paul's concerns.

Across the street, the crows lifted from the town hall roof as one, becoming a black, swirling cloud against the otherwise clear blue autumn sky.

"Shit," I muttered, and Paul's jaw dropped because the woman he wanted me to be wasn't supposed to swear, either.

Shit, shit, shit.

CHAPTER 2

"I HAVE TO GO." I STOOD UP FROM THE TABLE, MY HIPS protesting their time on the metal stool. "I have—things I need to do."

"But we haven't finished talking," Paul objected. "I haven't told you what Dr. Alvarado thinks."

The mention of my family doctor's name snagged my attention and almost made me pause. Almost. But the black cloud over the town hall swirled faster, and the wolf-shifter waiting outside had turned to frown at me through the plate-glass window separating us. Lucan might not be able to see the crows, but he had developed the uncanny ability to sense when I was the slightest bit uneasy or frustrated or out of sorts in any way. Time and again, he'd appeared at my side, no matter where I was in the house or the garden, aware within moments of my mood going off track, no matter what had triggered the change.

"—personality changes this big aren't normal—" Paul's voice floated along the edges of my focus. "—do an MRI to rule out a tumor—"

Still holding Lucan's gaze, I pointed out the window at the sky, and he turned to look upward. Then he pivoted back to me, scowling. *"Come,"* he mouthed at me. *"Now."*

Six weeks ago, I would have bristled at the high-handedness of the command. Now, I understood that it was rooted in his purpose. His drive to protect. I also wasn't anxious to face whatever the crows portended out here in the open like this. Every atom of my being cried out for the safety of the house in the woods, illusory as that safety was these days.

I reached for the staff I'd stood against the wall behind me, disentangling it from the fringe of a macramé wall-hanging. Lucan had carved it for me—the staff, not the wall-hanging—out of a branch of the linden tree that had saved me when the Mages had attacked with their goliath, and I never went anywhere without it. Not even out to the garden. Keven had rolled her eyes at the idea of a staff replacing the wand that the tree had grown from, but she hadn't argued with me about carrying it. We all knew my self-defense skills with a staff were far, far better than my magick. And if my magick ever *should* work? The staff would be like a wand on steroids.

I hoped.

"I'll call you in a few days," I cut across my son's continuing diatribe. Resting my free hand on his shoulder, I leaned down to kiss his cheek. "Give Braden a hug for me and tell him—"

Paul's hand fastened over my wrist. He pulled my hand away from his shoulder and gripped it in both of his. "For chrissake, Mom, would you *listen*? This is serious!" He swallowed, glanced around the crowded coffee shop, and dropped his voice to an earnest whisper. "We think there's something wrong with you. Dr. Alvarado wants you to come in to see her as soon as—"

In the grand scheme of elemental magick, what I did was little more than a parlor trick. But my connection to the Fire element was my most reliable—likely because, thanks to the return of post-menopausal hot flashes, I at least knew what I was trying to tap into—and trick or not, it had the intended effect. Paul's words dropped off mid-sentence, and he gaped at the ball of white flame seething in the palm of the hand I turned over in his grasp.

Edie groaned inside my head.

Careful to keep my body between it and the rest of the café, I ignored my friend's voice and willed the flame brighter, letting it rise until it hovered at the height of Paul's nose. The ball of fire was, much to Keven's ongoing dismay, as much as I'd managed to master, so far. As much as I'd been able to call forth before memories overwhelmed me and the connection dissolved into panic. But that wasn't important at the moment. All that mattered was that it be effective here and now, in this moment.

8

And, judging by the paling of Paul's face, it was. Almost cross-eyed, my son stared at the flame before him. His voice went hoarse. "Mom? What the hell..."

I flicked a glance out the window to be sure no passerby had noticed my impulsive display because, goddess, the repercussions could be bad. Then again, the repercussions of not doing it could be worse. Once my son got an idea into his head, it was all but impossible to disabuse him of it, and if he thought something was wrong with me, he wouldn't rest until he'd had me poked and prodded and tested for everything from tumors to Ebola.

And bad idea or not, it was done. I reabsorbed the flame into my hand and let the heat at my center dissipate.

"It's not a tumor," I told my son quietly. "You're right about me not being the same, but I'm not sick. I've just ... changed. And I have some things I need to take care of. I'll call you in a few days."

Paul recovered by the time I wound my way between the crowded tables to the door. Not one to miss out on having the last word—or to shy away from making a scene—he called, "We're not done, Mom. I'm not letting this go, damn it. You need to see the doctor. And for God's sake, would you please call your friend Jeanne? She keeps leaving messages at my office. Mom? Mom!"

Cheeks warm with embarrassment—although I honestly couldn't have said whether for me or my son—I left the Java Hut and let the door swing closed on his voice. Lucan fell into step beside me.

"So. Went well, did it?" he asked after a half-block or so.

"Paul doesn't much care for change," I said, keeping my answer vague.

"Or magickal displays, I'm guessing."

Guilt twinged, and I shot him a quick, sideways glance. "You saw."

9

"You're lucky no one else did. You took an enormous risk, milady."

"I know." I bit my lip and sighed. "And I'm sorry, but Paul's concerns were getting out of hand. He's been talking to his father—and to my doctor. I had to do *something*. You won't tell Keven, will you?"

My companion gave an amused snort. "You do know that *you* are the Crone, right? And the gargoyle is your servant?"

Crone. I still hadn't fully accepted that title. Not because of the negative connotations society bestowed on the term, but because of the enormous responsibilities they had no idea came with it. And not just for Crones with a capital 'c', either. All crones. All the 'women of a certain age' who did their part to hold together the very fabric of the same society that wanted nothing more to do with them, that wanted them to go away and be quiet and behave.

The way my own son did.

And that was without even knowing about the capital letter in my title.

"*He really is his father's son, isn't he?*" Edie grumbled. "*I should've given him more detentions.*"

"You—" I began, then bit off the rest of my "*gave him detentions?*" question when Lucan turned his head toward me. I hadn't yet figured out how to tell him—or Keven—about the conversations with my departed friend. I wasn't sure I wanted to. It was nice to have something of my former self that was still mine, even if she wasn't real. I just needed to remember to hold up my end of the conversation in my head.

"*I'm as real as you are, my friend,*" Edie's voice was tart. Then it softened. "*And I love you, too.*"

Blast. Now she was going to make me cry. I blinked back tears, and Lucan's brows twitched together.

"Milady?"

I shook my head. "It's nothing."

"And everything?" he suggested, too perceptive as always.

I didn't answer.

"The crows," he said after a moment. "Are they still with us?"

"Yes." I didn't have to look up to confirm it, because the murder had followed us, winging from tree to tree across the path of the autumn sun. Their shadows intermingled with ours as we headed down a tree-lined residential street toward the path that would take us back to the house in the woods.

"How many?"

"A lot."

So many more than I'd ever seen.

"It's going to be bad, isn't it?" Edie asked.

Yes. Yes, my friend, it's going to be bad.

"We should move faster," Lucan said, and his long legs carried him forward at a pace that had me scurrying to keep up.

I tugged the edges of my cloak closer against the October breeze that seemed suddenly chill despite the sun. One of these days, I would have to do something about getting a proper coat again. And boots. Boots would be good. Preferably before winter set in.

I looked up at the dark cloud of crows wheeling above us.

Assuming I lived long enough to see winter.

CHAPTER 3

THE MURDER CIRCLED THE STONE HOUSE AHEAD OF US three times as we crossed the clearing, then settled into the tree-tops on either side, perched in the skeletal maples and oaks that had shed their leaves in the advent of autumn. Trees that had slowly resurrected themselves in the month and a half since I'd leveled them with my loss of control. A testament to my Earth magick, Keven said, but I'm not sure any of us believed her. Least of all me.

Tight-lipped behind his beard, Lucan frowned over his shoulder at me, and I realized my steps had slowed. I knew I should catch up to him again, but instead I stopped altogether, my cloak held together with one hand and my ever-present staff in the other as I stared up at the corvids. The hairs on my arms and the back of my neck stood on end. Why were they so silent?

The chitter of a red squirrel drifted through the woods. It sounded angry, but red squirrels always sounded angry. Beyond that, from somewhere farther away, came the distant hammering of a woodpecker and the calls of wild geese winging high overhead.

But from the crows, not a sound.

The front door of the house opened, and I dropped my gaze to the massive stone gargoyle standing in the entrance and wiping her hands on a pink floral apron with a frilly pocket as she frowned out at us, a large ginger cat winding around her feet. Keven had chosen the fabric—well, she'd described what she wanted so I could buy it in town—and I'd made three aprons as a peace offering for her after a potion mishap (my fault) left her torso stained chartreuse for a week. I'd wanted something without ties that her chunky stone fingers would fumble with, so

12

they—the aprons, not her fingers—were pinafores. They were lopsided and not particularly well crafted, but she wore them anyway, and they salved my conscience a little.

Not a lot, but a little.

"What's wrong?" she asked in her gravelly voice, looking to Lucan for an answer rather than me. She'd done that a lot since that night six weeks ago—spoken to him rather than me whenever possible. And when she *did* need to speak to me, her words were sparse, her voice terse. I'd wondered once or twice if my continued magickal failures might be partly due to that, but somehow, I doubted it. I was plenty inept all on my own.

Lucan raised his voice to answer the gargoyle across the remainder of the clearing. "The crows are back."

Keven lumbered out to join us. Even though she wouldn't—couldn't—see the birds, she looked up at the trees, shading her eyes from the low afternoon sun with one hand. My gaze lingered on the roughened gap where she was missing a claw—another token of my inability to control the magick she had tried to teach me.

No wonder she found it hard to speak to me.

I sighed.

"How many?" she asked, dropping her hand and turning her head to me at last.

"A lot," I replied. "More than I've seen before."

She grunted and jerked her head toward the house. "It will be safer to talk inside."

I wanted to believe her, but I couldn't. Not when the house had all but fallen to the Mages once before. Not when the wards that had helped protect it then—whose kin I'd massacred—had refused to return since. Not when the chill that had taken up residence in my spine spread outward, curling like fingers around my insides. I tightened my grip on the staff, fighting to stay grounded in the here and now, and not let the memories rise. Not let the panic win.

13

I'm not ready, I wanted to tell my granite companion. *Whatever is coming, I'm not ready.*

But Keven already knew that. So did Lucan, to whom the gargoyle referred as the mutt—half in jest, half not so much because history. We all knew I wasn't ready. I had yet to master even the most basic spellcasting, and the fire I'd called to my palm in the coffee shop was the only elemental power I'd been able to summon since ... that night.

But we didn't talk about that. Not the night, not what I'd done, not how it had taken all three of us to drive away the goliath. And apart from Lucan's teasing comment on the way back from town, we certainly didn't talk about how I wasn't the Earth Crone that he and Keven had supposed me to be, but the until recently mythical Fifth Crone instead.

At least, no one talked about it with me. Between Keven and Lucan, however? I was fairly sure they talked about it a lot. About the as-yet to arrive Earth Crone they were supposed to serve. About my ongoing lack of control over the elements I was supposed to be able to connect with. About a lot of things I was equally sure I'd rather not know.

I stared up at the bare trees. The crows—far more than the fifty that had first visited me on the day all of this began—stared back. And if fifty had portended what had already happened, how much worse was coming now?

I'm not ready, I thought again as Keven trudged back toward the house. I waited for Edie's voice to pop up and reassure me, but she was notably silent. Because she wasn't there right now, or because she agreed? I closed my eyes, shutting out house and crows, gargoyle and wolf-shifter. Not for the first time—not by a long shot—I wanted to turn tail and run back to my old life. My simple life. My life where my son paid me dutiful weekly visits that were only a little grudging, where his wife fussed over my health (which was fine) and my advancing years (which were annoying but normal), and where my grandson followed me around my garden and peppered me

14

with incessant questions about the whys and the hows of the whole of the universe.

My old life that had disappeared first in flames when my house had burned down, and then in blood when I had killed. Not once, not twice, but three times.

Lucan cleared his throat. "Milady?" he prompted.

I opened my eyes. Keven had disappeared inside again with Mergan the cat, leaving the door open behind her. I lifted my chin and eased my cramped grip on the staff.

"Coming," I said and, with a last glance at the crow-peppered trees, followed him into the house.

Because there was no going back to a life that no longer existed.

AS SOON AS I WAS SAFELY IN THE HOUSE, LUCAN murmured something to the gargoyle waiting in the entry hall, morphed into his wolf form, and loped out the door—presumably on a scouting mission in the woods surrounding the house, because we had no wards to give us warning of anything approaching.

Keven closed the door behind Lucan and stomped down the hall toward the kitchen, leaving me—also presumably—to follow. Was it my imagination, or did she seem to do a lot of stomping these days? Or at least more than usual, given her granite composition.

I sighed and set off in her wake, arriving as she took off the pinafore and hung it on a hook by the door. I waited until she'd moved out of the way, then hung my cloak beside the pinafore and leaned my staff against the wall.

The scent of venison and herbs wafted through the air, and my mouth watered. As house gargoyle, Keven took her cooking role seriously, but her entire repertoire when I'd first arrived had extended only to stews and soups, with the occasional pot roast thrown in. (Which, let's face it, is just a dry version of stew.) Last week, however, I'd taught her how to make pastry, and now she'd added pot pies to her menu. Stew with a lid, she called it, and she had a point, but at least we had a little more variety. And it helped that her stews were excellent to begin with.

I took a seat on one of the benches along the harvest-style table as she placed a kettle of water to boil on the stove. Mergan jumped up beside me and butted his head against my elbow in a rare display of affection. He might have been my cat at one time, but ever since I'd brought him to the house with me, he had been firmly in the Keven-is-the-best-ever camp. Possibly related to me using his carrier as a sledgehammer against the gnomes that fateful night—with him in it.

Mergan bumped my elbow again, and I scratched around his ears as Keven took several jars of dried herbs down from the shelves. She worked in silence, and I chewed on my bottom lip as I watched. Gargoyles, I'd learned, weren't much for small talk, and Keven spoke only when she had something to say. Those somethings had become fewer and further between over the last few weeks. In this instance, I told myself that she was waiting for Lucan to join us so she could avoid having to repeat herself—rather than avoiding me—but I didn't believe me.

The scuff of boot against flagstone heralded my protector's return, and I looked over my shoulder as he came into the kitchen, pausing to sniff the air with an appreciation that echoed my own. Though I hoped I didn't have quite the same feral glint in my eye.

"Not that feral is all bad," Edie's voice mused in my head. *"You have to admit it's rather ... mmm."*

Her observation ended on what sounded like a purr, and I almost choked. But she was right, of course. With his usual man-bun back in place atop his head after his shift, my protector barely cleared the doorframe, he was broad enough that his shoulders did much the same, and the feral glint was definitely *mmm.* Even without Edie's help, my inner teenager made a point of noticing—every single time. And Lucan, damn his hide, always seemed to know.

A brief heat flared in the amber eyes that rested on me, but it was swiftly extinguished. Protectors, he had made it clear when we met, did not consort with those they protected. I believed him, but it didn't stop me from wishing it might be otherwise— and not just because of hormones, either. The level of comfort I felt in his company, the stillness and peace and *belonging* that I felt in my core—

Over by the stove, Keven growled. Or maybe cleared her throat. It was hard to tell sometimes, especially when she was scowling the way she was now. "Well?" she asked. "Anything?"

Lucan shook his head.

Keven frowned. "What do you suggest we do? Without the wards, we are ..." She trailed off, sending a look my way that I chose to interpret as frustration rather than utter despair.

I scuffed the toe of my running shoe against the flagstone floor under the table, wondering how she would have finished the observation if I hadn't been present. If the missing wards hadn't been my fault. *Sitting ducks? Up Shit Creek? Easy pickings?*

"We're more vulnerable than I would like," Lucan agreed, "but we're not without friends."

"The midwitches?" Keven asked.

I sat up straighter and shook my head. "No," I said. "I don't want to involve—"

"You and Lady Claire can shelter in the cellar until I return," Lucan said, as if I hadn't spoken. "In wolf form, I can be to town and back in half an hour."

"I'm not—" I said.

"And how will you pass the message?" Keven asked. "You're likely to be taken prisoner when you change back and you're not wearing any clothes."

"He's not—" I said.

"I'd be arrested if I were seen, not taken prisoner," Lucan

corrected, "but I won't be, because I won't need to change back. Kate will know something is up as soon as she sees my wolf."

I slapped both hands on the tabletop. "*Will* you both stop talking as if I'm not here!" I bellowed. Mergan bolted from the room. Gargoyle and shifter both turned their heads to stare at me. Crossing my arms, I tucked my burning palms against my ribs and donned my most ferocious scowl, partly because I felt ferocious, but mostly because damn it, that *hurt*.

I swallowed my whimper and prepared to read the two of them the riot act, because damn it again, Lucan was right. I *was* the Crone, and this was *my* house—at least for now—and *I* was supposed to be in charge, and it was about bloody time I—

Out in the front hall, the door crashed open, and a deep voice thundered through the house.

"Gargoyle!" it bellowed. "Attend my Crone!"

CHAPTER 4

LUCAN MORPHED INTO HIS WOLF FORM AND DISAPPEARED down the hallway before the shout's reverberations had died away, leaving his empty clothes to settle in the kitchen doorway. Keven made a grab for me, undoubtedly to stuff me into a cupboard for my own protection again, but the daily self-defense lessons Lucan subjected me to paid off in spades. With lightning reflexes and a grace I hadn't possessed in years—if ever—I evaded her stone claws and bolted after my protector.

I even remembered to grab my staff on my way.

Leaving Keven to growl at an empty kitchen, I sped down the flagstone corridor, arriving in the vaulted front entry seconds after Lucan. He had already changed back into a man and crouched, naked, over a prone woman on the floor. Another man, burly and heavily bearded, hovered beside him, bleeding from a dozen wounds.

Also naked.

My step hitched as acquired caution flared in me. The crows —had this been what they'd warned of? I gave my head a small shake and hurried forward. The crows' presence was undoubtedly connected, but I knew instinctively that our unexpected guests weren't the ones we needed to worry about.

"Attend my Crone," had been the bellow, which meant that this man was the unconscious woman's protector—her Lucan— and she needed help. I was two steps away when massive granite hands lifted me from the floor and set me to one side.

"Stay," Keven ordered. She lumbered past and crouched at the woman's side.

The stranger's eyes flashed between me and the gargoyle, and he frowned with what looked like a combination of surprise and outrage. At how Keven assumed control? Or at how I let her do so? The reasons behind both situations would take some explaining—*I* would take some explaining—but now was not the time. Not when the woman on the floor lay so still.

I peered over Keven's shoulder at her. She looked to be my age, or perhaps a little older. Long brown hair, heavily streaked with gray, framed a lined face. Her robe clung in tatters to shins scraped raw and caked in mud, and her feet were bare, filthy, and likewise injured. Worst of all, however, was her right arm, sticking out from her side at an angle that was all wrong.

Keven rose from her haunches. "Carry her to the fire," she directed Lucan. "And you"—she pointed at Burly Man—"to the kitchen with Lady Claire. Milady, his wounds are superficial. Can you manage?"

The bloody gash on the side of Burly Man's head, still seeping, looked anything but superficial to me, but I nodded. At the very least, I could clean and bandage it, and Keven could see to a healing potion later.

I motioned toward the hall leading to the kitchen, and Burly Man scowled. I thought he might refuse to follow, but Lucan lifted the woman from the floor and jerked his chin in my direction.

"Go," he told the other protector. "We've got her, and you'll just get in the way."

Burly Man hesitated another second, then snarled and stomped past me down the hallway, his bare feet slapping against the flagstones. I let out a breath I hadn't known I held.

"Chamomile and lavender?" I asked Keven as she followed Lucan and his burden toward the sitting room. Burly Man was going to need something to settle him. Keven glanced over her shoulder, her gaze going past me to where Burly Man had disappeared.

"Yes," she said. "Add skullcap and lemon balm, too. Extra skullcap."

Reluctantly—and not just because of the idea of tending to Burly Man—I left Keven and Lucan in the sitting room with their too-still patient. I made my way to the kitchen where I, too, would be out of their way. As much as I itched to do something to help, Keven's attempts at teaching me healing magick had gone about as well as my elemental lessons, and my best efforts now would be nothing more than a hindrance. From what I'd seen of the Crone, she needed every advantage right now. That arm ...

My step faltered outside the kitchen door. The arm had been only what was visible—that, and the scraped shins and feet. How much other damage had been inflicted on her? And by whom? Were they on their way here, now, following in the Crone's wake?

Was *that* what the crows warned of?

I shivered, my earlier chill returning. If it had ever left.

But one thing at a time. I had a patient of my own to see—

The kitchen door opened as I reached for the handle, and I stumbled forward, nearly face-planting on the floor. Burly Man watched me recover my footing, offering no help. Cheeks warm, I drew myself up to my full height—still several inches shorter than the large, naked stranger—and brushed past him into the room. I snagged Keven's pink-flowered pinafore off the hook on my way and wordlessly held it out to him.

Burly Man's his jaw flexed beneath his beard, but he snatched the garment from my hand and tugged it over his head. As he twitched the pinafore into place over the carpet of hair covering his chest, I noticed that his left arm ended in a scarred stump where his hand should have been. Burly Man looked up at the slight hitch in my breath. His gaze followed mine, and he grunted.

"An old battle wound," he said "I assure you it's no impediment to my performance, milady. In any of my ... activities."

The deliberate pause, combined with the upward tilt of one

bushy brow, made his meaning clear. As did the way his eyes traveled over my length. I felt my mouth fall open and snapped it shut again. Was he—? No. He couldn't be. Lucan had told me that protectors and their protectees couldn't ...

Maybe he'd meant only their own protectees?

But wait—did that mean that Lucan and another Crone might ...?

Burly Man's gaze traveled up to my face again. I brushed aside the questions I had no business asking—even internally—and pressed my lips together. I pointed to the bench beside the long, scarred wooden table.

"Sit," I ordered. I more than half-expected him to refuse, but with open amusement glinting in his gray eyes, he shrugged pink-flowered shoulders and settled on the bench. I turned my back on him, placed a kettle of water on the wood stove, and pulled random jars of herbs from Keven's shelves over the counter. Random, because Keven didn't label them, and I hadn't yet memorized their order. I would have to sniff the contents of each and hope I could identify the ones I sought.

"So," Burly Man said after a moment as I opened and closed jars. "You're the new Earth Crone."

"What makes—" I stopped and changed the question. "How do you know that?"

"I protect Water, and I've met Fire and Air already. And their protectors."

"Ah." Having selected the three most promising candidates, I measured the herbs into a teapot, doubling the amount of what I hoped was skullcap, as directed by Keven. My attempt at encouraging silence didn't work for long.

"You have an unusual relationship with your gargoyle."

"It's ... complicated," I allowed. "But it works."

He grunted. I stared at the wisp of steam rising from the kettle's spout. Did I dare try speeding up its process? The house seemed to shudder around me, and I decided not. Instead, I

A GATHERING OF CRONES

used the hand pump at the sink to fill a bowl with water and took a clean cloth from the shelf beneath, then carried both to the table. Burly Man raised both eyebrows.

"No healing potion?"

I gritted my teeth. "I want to clean the wound first and see how bad it is."

Another grunt. The water slopped over the bowl as I set it down, but I ignored it and turned my attention to his head wound. He sat without moving as I sponged it clean. He smelled of sweat and blood and fire, and I debated asking what had happened, but I wasn't sure I wanted to invite conversation.

My thoughts returned to my next move. I couldn't make a healing potion to save my own life, but admitting that probably wasn't my best option, given the number of questions the confession would invite. I wasn't altogether sure what an Earth Crone could do, but it was a fair bet she could at least do that. Given Keven's disappointment in my lack of success during lessons, I suspected all Crones could do at least basic healing. And likely midwitches, too. And lesser witches, for that matter.

Yup. Option one would definitely bring too many questions.

Option number two would be to fake it, I supposed. I knew Keven kept a jar of heal-all in the pantry, along with several other ready-made lotions and potions, but they were also unlabeled, and my chances of choosing the right one were slim to none. With my luck, I'd pick something that burned the skin right off Burly Man, and—

His hand closed over mine. Our gazes locked. His was not friendly.

"Who are you?" he growled from between gritted teeth.

My mouth flapped, but no sound emerged—in part, because my throat had closed, but mostly because my brain synapses had stopped firing altogether. I had nothing—including air in my lungs. Burly Man's glower deepened, and his grip tightened on my wrist.

23

"Leave her be, Bedivere," Lucan's voice commanded from the kitchen doorway. "Lady Claire is under my protection."

For an instant, I didn't think Burly Man—Bedivere?—would listen, but after another tightening of his hold on me that threatened to snap my wrist bones, he threw my hand aside. I wasted no time in stepping out of reach, although if he moved as fast as I knew Lucan did, the paltry distance between us would buy me a nanosecond at best. My heart—now lodged at the base of my throat—beat an uncomfortable staccato.

Lucan quirked an eyebrow at me. "Are you all right?"

My voice still didn't work, so I nodded. He turned his attention back to Bedivere, who had risen from the bench. His lips twitched.

"Nice outfit."

Bedivere ignored the jibe. "She is not Crone."

"She is."

"I have been serving the Crones for fourteen centuries. They do not behave the way she does. She acts like she's afraid of her own shadow."

"I've been serving the Crones for the same time," Lucan reminded him, "and it's complicated. But now is not the time to go into it. *Your* Crone has recovered consciousness. She's asking for you."

Again, I thought Bedivere might not listen. Belatedly, it occurred to me that I should have made him drink the tea before I'd gone anywhere near him.

After a long last glare at me that sat somewhere between hostile and more hostile, he spun on his heel and pushed past Lucan into the hallway beyond. There, he paused and looked back at my protector, and his expression softened to almost-not antagonistic.

"Circumstances aside, it is good to see you again, brother," he said gruffly.

Lucan reached out and gave his shoulder a brief squeeze. "And you. Now go to your Crone. We'll talk later."

"Brother?" I asked in the silence that followed Burly Man's departure. Bedivere. I vaguely recognized the name, but my knowledge of Arthurian legend was rusty. I wondered if it was something I needed to brush up on, or if I would find the knowledge included in the *Crone Wars* book that I hadn't been able to—

"We shared a mother," Lucan's answer interrupted my thought. "You're sure you're okay?"

My nod was jerky, but at least it was still a nod. "He's very ... intense, your brother."

"Not all of the protectors found it easy to adapt to the changes we've faced in the world since Camlann. Some of us— including Bedivere—prefer to exist in their wolf-form between Crones. It makes them ..."

The word *wild* sprang to my mind when he trailed off, and I shivered.

"There's more," Lucan said. He leaned a shoulder against the doorframe and crossed his arms. "At the very beginning, when the Morrigan created the pendants, Morok thought he could simply take them by force. We managed to keep the Crones out of his reach for a time, but eventually, he got lucky."

I stopped breathing. "Morok killed a Crone?"

"He did. She was the only one we've ever lost, and Bedivere never recovered. As driven by magick as we all are to protect our Crones, he is driven by more. He's never forgiven himself for Lady Isabelle's death."

"And ... her pendant?"

"Vanished into the aether. It was a safeguard built in by the Morrigan that none of us knew about until then. If one of the Crones is killed by Morok's hand—or by one of his Mages—the pendant disappears until it can choose its next Crone. Unless a Crone gives up her pendant voluntarily, she must die of natural causes before it is freed from her. And unless Morok knows where to find her at the moment of her death, the pendant remains out of his reach."

It was on the tip of my tongue to ask why no one had thought to tell me any of this before—at least beyond the voluntary handover part—but I suspected it was all in the *Crone Wars* book I hadn't yet figured out how to read. And because I'd rather not open up *that* line of discussion again, I opted for another question.

"So the Mages—their attacks—what's the purpose of those, if it's not to kill us?"

"Oh, their intent is still to kill, milady," Lucan assured me, his amber eyes somber. "Never doubt that for a second. If they cannot get their hands on the pendants, their only other choice is to stop the Crones from using them to raise the power to split the world again—any way they can."

Ah. Well, then. Awesome.

"And now"—Lucan straightened away from the doorframe —"I must get back to the others."

And I wasn't invited, of course. I squelched my petty hurt feelings. "How is the Water Crone?"

"Badly injured, but the gargoyle is very good at what she does."

"Unlike her pupil," my Claire-voice observed primly.

Goddess, but I was beginning not to like that part of myself very much.

"Do we know what happened?"

Lucan's head shook. His man-bun had come undone again in his shift, and his hair lay across his shoulders in the wild tangle that always made my fingers itch to comb through it and straighten it out. I wondered, not for the first time, why he didn't just cut it. But, also not for the first time, I concluded that the question wasn't important enough to ask.

"Can I do anything?" I said instead, already knowing the answer but asking anyway because—what the hell?—I might as well feel even more useless. I folded my arms across myself in anticipation of the answer.

Lucan walked across the kitchen to the door leading to the

garden, bolted it, and dropped the wooden bar into place across it.

"Stay here," he said, and then he went back to join the others.

Exactly as I'd expected.

CHAPTER 5

I ENDED UP DRINKING THE TEA I'D MADE FOR BEDIVERE myself.

I sat in the kitchen, alone with my skittering thoughts and the heavy silence of Lucan's abandonment, because he *had* abandoned me. Maybe not fully, and maybe not yet, but complete abandonment was coming. It was inevitable.

Because Fifth Crone, I'd realized today, roughly translated to *fifth wheel.*

"She's not Crone." Bedivere's words went round and round in my head.

And worse, Lucan's response: *"It's complicated."*

No introduction of me as Fifth Crone. No vehement defense such as a Crone might expect of her protector. Just ... *complicated.*

And it was. More so than I'd wanted to admit before now.

More than the hard knot in the pit of my stomach still wanted to admit.

But with the Crones beginning to gather—and if there were three of them, the fourth was out there somewhere—I could no longer avoid the fact that soon, I would have no place. Because *complicated* included untidy little facts such as this being the Earth Crone's house—not mine. Which made Lucan her protector and Keven her servant—not mine. Things I hadn't had to think about before. Or, more accurately, that I hadn't *wanted* to think about. The knot in my stomach twisted, and I closed my eyes and dropped my forehead onto my arms, folded across the worn tabletop.

I'd had a hard enough time facing this bloody Crone destiny *with* the backing of my wolf-shifter protector and my walking, talking gargoyle. What in the name of the goddess would I do without them? Especially when I couldn't magick my way out of a paper bag to save my own life? Or anyone else's, for that matter.

Not since that night.

"I don't stand a chance," I mumbled into the table.

An inner voice gave a beleaguered sigh and asked, *"Are we back to that again?"*

Edie had returned, and her voice held the *prepare for a lecture* tone that was a holdover from her former career as a high school principal. I was in no mood.

"Go away," I growled.

"Oh, my. Someone's knee-deep in self-pity."

I lifted my head from my arms, remembered I couldn't see her, and let it drop again.

If I ignored her, maybe she would leave and let me wallow in—

The sound of liquid pouring made me jolt upright, my every nerve on high alert at the possibility Bedivere had returned to continue his interrogation. But the room remained empty except for me and the unmanned teapot settling back onto the table beside my cup. I gaped at it. Cheesy rice—

"I've been practicing," Edie said smugly.

"Why?" I grumbled. "So you can better haunt me?"

"No. So I can pour you tea when you need a friend." Her voice was tart.

Somewhat abashed by my churlishness, I mumbled an apology, then waved a hand over the teapot, still half-expecting to find invisible wires. "How—?"

Silence. Exasperated silence, if I interpreted it correctly. Because duh.

"Magick," I answered my own unfinished question. "But ..."

"I'm dead, not gone, Claire. Magick is energy, I'm energy. It's not that difficult, once you get the hang of it."

More silence. My self-pity returned, well past knee-deep this time.

"Sure," I said finally. "I'll remember that the next time I try to use it."

Edie sighed. *"Drink the tea,"* she said.

I lifted the cup to my lips.

"Milady?" Lucan's voice in the kitchen doorway made me jump, and tea sloshed down the front of my shirt, soaking through to my skin. I yelped and plucked the scalding fabric away from my chest, then looked over to find him frowning at the otherwise empty kitchen. He turned his gaze back to me. "Who were you talking to?"

"My—"

"Don't," Edie whispered.

"—self," I said, which was what I'd started to say in the first place. "I was talking to myself. I do that sometimes." I reached for a tea towel to dab at my wet shirtfront and the ever-present pendant beneath it. "Did you want something?"

"Lady Anne wants to meet you."

"Now?" I looked up mid dab.

"Unless you have something more pressing?" Lucan surveyed the kitchen again. One brow lifted above enigmatic amber eyes.

I could think of a hundred things I would personally consider more pressing than facing the Water Crone—a *real* Crone, who would no doubt see me for the imposter I increasingly felt like, and who would be accompanied by Burly Man—but I doubted Lucan would agree that any of them were reasonable excuses. Besides, I supposed there wasn't much point in avoiding the meeting, or the reckoning that would surely follow. I set the tea towel on the table, downed the rest of my calming tea in one gulp, and pasted a sad imitation of a smile on my lips.

"Ready," I lied.

FLAMES BLAZED HIGH IN THE SITTING ROOM FIREPLACE. The Water Crone lay on one of the couches flanking it—the same one Lucan had occupied after defending me from the shade's attack on my first night in the house, and on which I'd lain myself after the gnome bit me.

I hesitated in the doorway, assessing the woman propped up on pillows. Mergan had made himself at home on the blanket over her lap, and Keven had washed her and helped her to change—or, more probably, changed her, because I didn't think she would have been able to do much herself, given the number of bruises and lacerations visible now that the layers of grime were gone. Her broken arm had been splinted and lay on top of the blankets covering her, and her brown eyes were clouded with pain and exhaustion. But they were still astute as they met mine. I tightened my lips, suspecting Bedivere had wasted no time in voicing his opinion of me.

The Water Crone's gaze dropped to the pendant resting on my chest—a crystal magnifying lens in an ornate silver surround. She lifted her other hand from the cat she'd been petting and gestured at the pendant.

"May I?" she asked.

I hesitated. I hadn't taken the pendant off in weeks—not even to bathe or sleep. Not since—

I looked to Lucan for direction, but he stood in the shadows by the fireplace, his features unreadable. My gaze slid to Keven, who inclined her head in tacit agreement with the Water Crone's request. I lifted the crystal from around my neck and stepped toward the couch, only to come up short against a solid wall of hairy chest covered in pink flowers. Instantly, Lucan was by my side.

"Bedivere!" he snarled.

The chest growled back in response, vibrating against me, but after a tense, nose-tickling moment, Bedivere stepped back enough to let me squeeze past. Just.

The Water Crone, who had said nothing, held out her hand and I placed my pendant in her palm, feeling naked and vulnerable without its familiar weight around my neck. She studied it for a long time, turning it over and over in her fingers, her expression giving away nothing of her thoughts. Then, without comment, she handed it back to me.

I looped the pendant's chain over my head again. I opened my mouth to ask the Water Crone if I might sit, remembered it was my house, remembered it *wasn't* actually my house, wondered if—

"For goddess' sake, sit!" Edie's voice hissed in my head.

I firmed my lips, squared my shoulders, and walked around the wooden trunk that served both as storage for Keven's always-ready supply of blankets and as a coffee table between the two sofas. What was *with* me? I hadn't been this indecisive in months. Not since my ex had left, and I'd finally stopped feeling like an interloper in my own home. My former home. My former life.

Ah.

"Yes, 'ah,'" said Edie.

Oh.

I took a deep breath. Apparently, I still had some unpacking to do with regards to that former life, but later. For now, in light of the Earth Crone's absence and the events that had brought me here, I supposed the house was as much mine as anyone's. I looked across at the other woman, searching for something to say and settling on a basic introduction. She probably knew my name already, thanks to Burly Man, but we had to start somewhere. I perched on the edge of the sofa across from the woman.

"My name is Claire," I said. "Claire Emerson."

"Anne Stillwater," the Water Crone responded. "Ironic, yes?"

I tried to smile. "A little, perhaps. How is your arm?"

"It will heal. Your gargoyle—" Sadness flashed across her features, and she broke off, then recovered. "Your gargoyle is highly skilled."

I hesitated, loath to probe what I suspected was an open wound of another kind. But the question sat between us, and the lines around Anne's mouth deepened.

"Mine did not survive the attack," she said.

A low groan came from the corner of the room into which Keven had retreated, rough as the rock from which she was made, pained as Anne's expression. I remembered the gargoyle's gruff sympathy when she'd learned of Edie's death. *"I, too, have lost friends,"* she'd said, and now she had lost another.

"I'm sorry," I said, and I hoped Keven knew my words encompassed her as well.

Anne, who had glanced around in surprise at Keven's sound of grief, turned back to me and lifted the shoulder of her uninjured arm. The blanket slid from it. "Perhaps if the other gargoyles had been there with us ..."

"No, milady," Bedivere interjected with a shake of his bearded head. With a tenderness that surprised me, given what I'd seen of him so far, he drew the blanket up again with his one hand and tucked it around her, ignoring the cat that hissed at him from her lap. "Nothing could have stood against that thing. We were lucky to escape it alive."

"Wait—the others were with you?" Lucan asked. "All of them?"

"All but Earth. We were waiting for her when they struck," Bedivere replied. "A half-dozen mages, twice that number of shades, and the goliath. We didn't stand a chance. The Water house fell within minutes, and it was all I could do to get the Lady Anne out of there and into the ley line that brought us here. I have no idea if the others made it."

My heart faltered and threatened to stop beating altogether. Earth was missing, and Fire and Air might be dead? Dear goddess, if that were true—

I folded my hands together in my lap, clinging tightly as I stared at them and willed the surge of panic in my belly to subside. If that were true, it would leave me and a severely injured Anne to take on goddess knew how many shades and mages, and that *thing*. The monster Lucan had called an unfortunate merging of gargoyle and wolf-shifter.

And on the extremely remote—no, make that impossible—chance that we prevailed, there would still be Morok himself.

Lucan cleared his throat. My gaze flashed to him, and I frowned. Why was he looking so apologetic? His shoulders hunched, his amber eyes slid away from mine, his—

Oh hell, no.

I held out a hand to stop the words I knew were coming, shaking my head in silent appeal. *Don't*, I thought. *Please don't tell them. Not yet.*

He either didn't understand or chose to ignore me. I suspected it was the latter.

"It attacked here as well," he said. "The goliath, along with three mages."

Bedivere wheezed his surprise. "Here? This house? But you're still here." He looked up at the beams crossing the ceiling. "And the house—"

"It was six weeks ago," said Lucan. "The house has had time to repair itself, and we've had time to heal."

"Repair! Heal?" Bedivere gaped, and I was a little open-jawed myself. The house repairs had all taken place at night. I'd assumed Keven had done them, because while gargoyles might get hungry, they seemed never to tire, and Keven had no bedchamber. It had never occurred to me that the house itself might—

On the other hand, it should have been obvious because again ... always ... magick.

"It *decimated* the Water house, Lucan," Bedivere said. "There was nothing left *to* repair. And if we hadn't left—" He broke off and stared at me suspiciously from beneath warring, bushy brows. "How?" he demanded.

"I—" My mouth flapped, but no further sound emerged. I fought the urge to scurry into the shadows and retreat behind Keven's bulk—in part because I didn't trust my legs to get me that far, but mostly because Bedivere stood in the way, and something about the raw energy rolling off him scared the living daylights out of me.

"How?" he snarled again, making me jump in my seat.

"Enough, Bedivere," Anne said quietly. "I'd like to speak alone with Claire."

"But, milady—"

"I'll be fine. Go. The gargoyle will make you something to eat, and Lucan will find you clothes."

Bedivere directed another scowl my way, and it took every ounce of willpower I possessed not to bolt for the door. Or at least crawl under a couch cushion.

But at last, he turned his attention to the Water Crone and nodded acquiescence. "As you wish, milady. Call if you need me."

CHAPTER 6

ANNE WASTED NO TIME IN GETTING TO THE POINT.
"Bedivere says you're not the Earth Crone," she said when the
door had snapped shut behind the others. Her gaze was steady.
Speculative. But—at least so far—not accusing.

"No," I said. "I'm not."

"But the pendant"—she nodded across the trunk at the
crystal laying on my chest—"is a Crone's pendant."

"Yes."

"And you defeated the goliath."

I swallowed in an effort to bring moisture to the desert that
used to be my mouth. "Defeated would be stretching it."

Letting her head rest against the pillows that Keven—or
perhaps the softer side of Bedivere—had propped behind her,
she studied me in silence, a tiny pucker between her brows.

"I didn't think you'd be real," she said at last. "At least, not in
my lifetime."

I didn't pretend not to understand. "You know about—" I
broke off, unable—unwilling—to voice the *me* that ended the
question. That sounded pretentious at the very least, if not
downright arrogant.

"All midwitches—and Crones—know about the Fifth." Her
brows puckered again. "But *you* should know that, too."

My gaze slid away. "It's ..."

My voice trailed into a silence that stretched between us,
broken by the crackle and snap of the fire, the rumble of
Mergan's contented purr, the soft rub of skin against skin as I
twisted my hands together. Because *complicated* didn't even
begin to cover it.

I reached my thoughts out to Edie, in need of a little moral
support. But my friend was either absent again or choosing to

remain silent—I had no way of telling which—and I was on my own.

"Tell me," Anne said.

And because I couldn't escape doing so, I did. Haltingly and without looking at her, I confessed my shortcomings as a Crone. I told her how the pendant had come into my life on my sixtieth birthday. How I had found the house—and Lucan and Keven; how I'd learned that magick was real—and fought the discovery; how I'd had no training or experience beyond my own fumbling —and brief—foray into Wicca years before.

"Well," she said when I finished. Then she fell silent, staring into the fire's dancing flames.

I waited for more, studying her across the wooden chest, noting the drawn lines around her mouth. What must she think, this Water Crone who had escaped the mages and their monster, only to discover the help she sought was all but non-existent?

"Well," she said again. Then, "*No* magickal training?"

I shook my head. "Keven's been trying to teach me, but—"

"Keven?"

"The gargoyle."

"Your gargoyle has a name?" She waved away the question. "Never mind that for now. Go on. But what?"

Her gargoyle *hadn't* had a name? I filed the question away— along with the many others I had—for later and picked up my story.

"But without the ..." I trailed off. I hadn't even told Keven about my issues with the book. I'd just kept trying. At first, I thought I just needed my reading glasses, but that turned out not to be the problem. I'd squinted, turned it this way and that, tried various angles and lights, pleaded with it, sworn at it, and done everything I could think of, but all without success. As far as I could tell, it wasn't even written in English—it was just a bunch of squiggles that I was supposed to be able to read as a Crone ... and couldn't.

"Without what?" Anne prompted.

My lips pulled tight. If confession was supposed to be so good for the soul, why did it feel like I was ripping out my heart with my own hands? I rubbed at the ache in the center of my chest. The hollowness. "I haven't been able to read the book," I admitted. "The grimoire."

"The one that came with the house?"

I nodded.

"Of course not. It's not yours to read."

"It's—what?"

Anne pressed her lips together and stared at me a moment in obvious consternation at my utter dearth of knowledge. Then she shook her head as if to clear it.

"There are four books," she said. "Each can be read only by the Crone to whom it belongs. If this is the Earth Crone's house, as it must be, it stands to reason that the book is hers as well."

I digested the news, relieved that this particular failure wasn't actually my fault, irritated that no one had told me about this aspect of the book until now, and all too aware of the return of the hard knot in my chest. Because now I was not only to have no house, no gargoyle, and no protector, but no book, either? Awesome. Just awesome.

I focused on my irritation because it seemed least likely to make me cry.

Anne gave a wan smile. "Don't be too hard on your gargoyle," she said. "She's only ever served one of the four. She wouldn't even know about the book's limitations."

"And Lucan?"

"Not his purview. His sole purpose is one of protection."

Protection of the Earth Crone. The knot grew, and my mood spiraled further downward. Six weeks I'd spent trying—and failing—to read that damned book. Six weeks of dodging Keven's questions about it, convinced there was something wrong with me, feeling like more of an imposter every day, afraid Keven and Lucan would find out and abandon me. Certain now that they would do exactly that.

"So," Anne said, grimacing as she shifted her weight again. "You've told me what you can't do. Why don't you tell me what you *can* do?"

"Are you sure you want to know? Shouldn't you rest?" I waved a vague hand at her battered body.

"I'm sure I need to know." She ignored my rest suggestion, and I didn't press the matter. She knew her limits better than I, and given she'd come here expecting some kind of assistance, it seemed only fair that she have the full picture of my limitations.

I drew my knees up to my chest—marveling yet again at the renewed flexibility that had come with Lucan's self-defense lessons—and hugged them against me as I rested my chin on them. They would make a poor barrier against the disappointment I knew to be imminent, but the position helped, nonetheless. I cleared my throat.

"I can see crows," I said. "They're harbingers, I think. I see them when something is coming or going to happen, but I never know what it is until it arrives or happens. And I can connect with all the elements, but not reliably. And not with any control."

"*Could connect,*" said my Claire-voice. "*Past tense.*"

"*Piss off,*" Edie told it.

So. She *was* here and choosing to remain silent while I fended for myself. Some friend.

"*You know I'm right,*" my Claire-voice said. "*You haven't been able to—*"

I shut out both voices and tried to keep my attention on the only real person speaking.

"When you say not with any control ..." Anne trailed off, waiting for details.

I unwrapped my arms from around my legs long enough to tick off my "accomplishments" on my fingers. "I blew a hole in the side of my house—my old house, not this one. I created a storm that knocked Keven off her feet and just about destroyed the cellar. I grew a tree from my linden wand right through the foundation. And I swamped the house and damn near drowned myself."

One of her eyebrows lifted, then dropped to join the other in a frown. "I see," she murmured. "No wonder the house feels on edge."

She could feel its wariness, too? Wonderful.

"Is that all? What about when the mages attacked? What happened then?"

I hugged my knees close again. Hadn't I told her enough already? I didn't want to talk about the attack. I didn't want to remember. I didn't want to be ...

I swallowed against the burn of bile rising in my chest. Tiny lights flickered along the edges of my vision, and the world narrowed until it felt like I was at one end of a long tunnel with Anne waiting at the other end. Waiting and judging and—

I inhaled, and the air sliced my throat like shards of broken glass. "I killed them," I whispered thickly, saying it aloud for the first time since that night. "I killed the mages, I flattened the forest, and I destroyed thousands of wards—and I still have no idea how."

I knew only that I didn't want to be the kind of person who was capable of wreaking such devastation.

MY WORDS OF CONFESSION WERE STILL HANGING HEAVY IN the air between us when the sitting room door opened and Keven entered, balancing two mugs in one hand. With no apology for the intrusion, she crossed the room to set one of the mugs, steam rising from its pale-yellow contents, on the trunk before me. It landed with a distinct *thunk*, as if carrying the weight of the gargoyle's disapproval, though I wasn't sure what I'd done—this time—to earn the censure.

Keven turned to help Anne into a sitting position. She

handed a second mug to her, waited to make sure the Water Crone's grip on the vessel was secure, and then straightened.

"You should rest soon, milady," she told Anne. She didn't look my way, but her words held an oblique accusation directed at me. "Your injuries need time to heal."

Ah. That was it. Or part of it, anyway.

"I will," Anne replied. "Soon."

The gargoyle *harumphed* and lumbered out of the room again, and I watched her close the door behind her, all without so much as a glance in my direction. That she held me responsible for preventing Anne's rest I understood, but this was more. It was ...

"*The beginning of the end,*" my Claire-voice suggested, and I suspected she was right. The ache in the middle of my chest turned raw. Was this what it was to be like now that a true Crone had arrived to take control? Would Lucan's behavior toward me change, too? I pressed a hand over my breastbone. It didn't help.

Anne cleared her throat. "So," she said. "What do you want to do?"

It wasn't the question I was expecting after my revelations. I blinked at her. "Do?"

She lifted her teacup, caught her breath, exhaled slowly, then sipped the liquid, her hand trembling with the effort of holding it to her lips. She lowered it again to her lap, where Mergan sniffed at it before returning to his eyes-closed loafing. Then she looked across at me. Her gaze was steady, but I sensed shadows lurking beneath her seeming calm.

"If the others don't find their way here before I'm healed, I'll need to go after them. I could use your help."

I blinked again. Was she more injured than I'd realized? Delirious? Delusional? "Did you not hear what I said about no control? If we end up in a battle, I'm more likely to kill you—or the others—by accident than I am to be of help."

"I can teach you," she said. "Not everything, of course, and not right away. I'll need a day or two to rest first, but I can at least show you how to connect with Water. Perhaps you can extrapolate from there—use the same methods to reach the other elements."

My entire body tensed. I took a moment to coax my muscles to unwind enough so that I could at least breathe. My first instinct, especially in the face of the freshly revisited memories of my many and spectacular failures, was to reject the suggestion outright. But surely having another Crone as my teacher instead of a gargoyle would make a difference.

Keven was the first to admit to having limited knowledge of magick in general and to not understanding elemental connections at all. And Edie, bless her departed heart and valiant attempts, hadn't had any success in teaching me, either—in part because she couldn't physically demonstrate things to me, and I, apparently, couldn't follow verbal instructions worth shit. And in greater part because, my friend had said gently, if something went wrong—if *I* went wrong—she would be unable to mitigate the damage.

Surely, however, a Crone would be able to show me how to connect reliably to the elements ... wouldn't she?

"But what if you connect and you still can't control it?" whispered my Claire-voice. Another voice sighed in exasperation.

"You know, that old-you-voice gets really annoying after a while," Edie said tartly.

She was right. But so was my Claire-voice. A chill slipped over my shoulders. I glanced toward the fireplace. The fire was getting low in its grate, and Keven hadn't stoked it when she brought the tea. Nor had she given me a blanket, as she once would have done.

"Well?" Anne prompted.

"What if I can't be taught?" I asked. "What if ..." I trailed off, not wanting to give voice to the question I was sure she wondered herself, now that she'd met me. The question I was sure we all asked ourselves.

What if I've been the wrong choice for Fifth Crone all along?

Because with every passing day, with every failure, and now with Anne's arrival, it had become increasingly difficult to turn away from the possibility that I was just that. A mistake. A giant, goddess-made miscalculation. An epic blunder of potentially cosmic proportions.

The Water Crone, however, spoke not with judgment, but with an unexpected compassion. "This must feel incredibly over-whelming," she said. "I know how unprepared *I* felt when my pendant came to me, and I'd spent a lifetime studying the craft. I can't imagine how much of a shock it was to you—or how exhausted you must be from trying to learn everything you need to know."

I blinked back a sheen of tears, suddenly aware of the weight across my shoulders that I'd been carrying—and trying so hard to ignore—for the past six weeks. Exhausted didn't begin to describe how I felt. I realized I didn't so much want to run away as I just wanted to curl up in a ball and cry. I was sixty years old, faced with a responsibility I'd never asked for—a task I couldn't pretend to understand, never mind undertake, and—

A weight settled onto the couch beside me. I jumped, then realized that the Water Crone had somehow gotten up from her couch, maneuvered past the trunk, and joined me on my sofa—injuries and all. And I hadn't even noticed. Shock, guilt, and concern all twisted through me at once, snapping me out of my self-pity.

"Oh my god, Anne—you shouldn't be moving around like that! Keven will have my head if she finds out." And I didn't even want to think about what Burly Man would do to me.

Fortunately for both of us, Anne didn't expire on the spot from her exertions. She even managed a smile as, with her good arm, she extended the blanket she wore across her shoulders and wrapped it around me as well, giving me a reassuring squeeze in the process.

"I'll teach you," she said again, "and we'll do the best we can. Together."

"And if that's not enough?"

"It will be."

But other words hung unspoken in the air between us. Heavy words that detracted from her promise and her seeming confidence. That undermined my own. That loomed like a dark, foreboding cloud.

It has to be.

Because the alternative didn't even bear thinking about.

CHAPTER 7

ANNE'S RECOVERY TOOK LONGER THAN THE DAY OR TWO she'd predicted. Despite the urgency behind getting my magick operational—not to mention finding the other Crones—it was four days before she was well enough to begin teaching me. Four long, almost entirely silent days.

On the first morning, I went down to the kitchen for breakfast as usual, only to find that Lucan and Keven had already eaten, and Keven had set my place in the dining room, rather than at the worn harvest table I'd shared with them since my arrival. The meal set the tone for the others that followed—and for the days in their entirety.

Keven and Lucan ate in the kitchen, sometimes with Bedivere, and I ate alone at the long, empty table, listening to the murmur of words I couldn't quite hear, interspersed with the occasional shout of laughter. When I finished pushing my food around my plate and pretending I was hungry, I would emerge to find Lucan gone and Keven engrossed in kitchen or cleaning tasks. She made no effort to continue my training—not even in potions or herbs—and stood still, without speaking unless spoken to, whenever I entered a room she was in.

By the afternoon of the second day, I found myself avoiding her just as much as she avoided me, because it just seemed easier that way.

I did have one conversation with Lucan on the second morning. It involved a brief, awkward exchange of pleasantries in the corridor outside the kitchen. Brief, because he kept sidling toward the front entry while grunting one-word answers to my questions, as if he had somewhere more important to be. Awkward, because it was clear that, wherever that somewhere might be, I wasn't welcome.

It left me with a vague feeling of redundancy, like I no longer fit into what I'd begun to think of as my home—or into Lucan's life. I did my best to convince myself that it was all in my head, but I didn't believe me.

I stopped seeing Lucan at all, after that. I didn't pass him in the hall, didn't see him emerge from the kitchen at mealtimes, didn't so much as catch a glimpse of him in the distance. It was as if he wasn't even in the house. In his absence, my sparring lessons stopped, and my days stretched out before me like empty fields that needed to be crossed but went on forever. I practiced my staff work on my own in the clearing, just to give myself something to do, but it wasn't the same without him, and my sessions were half what he would have insisted I do. He didn't check up on me. Didn't correct me. Didn't once respond to the changes in my mood the way he had before Anne's arrival.

I missed that most of all.

And my mood wasn't helped by the presence of his brother.

Silent and scowling, Bedivere watched me from a window if I was outside, from the top of the stairs when I came back in, from the kitchen doorway when I finished my meal and left the dining room. I took to tiptoeing up the back stairs to my bedchamber in the evenings so I wouldn't have to pass his wolf curled up in the hallway outside the Water Crone's door. He still growled his opinion of me whenever I stepped into the corridor, however. Just to be sure I remembered, perhaps?

I didn't know, and as the days wore on, I increasingly didn't care.

By the morning of day five, I'd had enough. Not even Edie had been around to alleviate my utter boredom, and frustration already seethed in my core when I woke. I stared at the ceiling as the night's shadows slowly gave way to dawn, pondering the day stretching ahead of me, as empty as the last four had been. Days that reminded me altogether too much of my pre-Crone life, when I'd existed in the kind of limbo that came with waiting for other people to live their lives before I made a decision or choice of my own. All so I could fit in around them. Support them. Not get in their way.

When I'd tiptoed up metaphorical back stairs every day in order to avoid confrontations.

All of which had a lot to do with how I'd ended up divorced and lacking purpose in my life, I suspected. And with how my son had become entirely too like his father for anyone's good. I threw off the covers that were suddenly too warm. Stifling.

Well, no more. No more waiting around, no more avoiding conflict, and no more—

"No more Ms. Nice Guy?" Edie inquired.

Trust her to turn up now, when I'd already solved my problem without her help. Unless ...

I frowned, half-focused on Edie, half on the hot flash threatening to wash over me.

"Go ahead," my friend encouraged. *"You're almost there."*

"You disappear on purpose," I accused the room, "so that I have to figure things out for myself."

"Ding, ding, ding!" she yelled. *"Give the lady a prize! It's called personal growth, by the way, and you're welcome."*

"And you," I growled, swinging my legs out of bed as the hot flash—thankfully—retreated, "are becoming more of a pain in the ass every day. How long are you planning on haunting me, anyway? Isn't there a ghostly time limit or something?"

"I'm not a ghost," she said smugly.

"What then?"

"I'm an ancestor, my friend. One of thousands."

"But we aren't—weren't—related."

"Not the bloodline kind of ancestors. Witch ancestors. All the witches that have gone before you."

I paused, halfway through putting on my pants. "Come again?"

"The third voice you hear sometimes? That's them. Us. Collectively."

Awesome. It wasn't bad enough that I had her and my

Claire-voice running amok in my brain, now I had thousands of others residing there as well?

Edie chuckled. *"Oh, Claire. You kill me sometimes."*

I wheezed, feeling like I'd just run headfirst into a concrete wall. It had been my house Edie had died in, and me who should have died, and I didn't think I would ever come to terms with—

My friend snorted. *"You know that's not what I meant."*

I did, but the words had been sobering, nonetheless. I'd been about to march downstairs and start throwing my weight around, demanding my rightful place as Crone, all because I was —what? Bored? How could I have so easily forgotten the consequences of my actions? The number of people who tended to die when I acted without thinking? I let my pants drop to the floor, leaned my elbows on my knees, and buried my face in my hands.

Cheesy rice on a—

"Oh, goddess, are we back to that again?" Edie groaned. *"It was a stupid thing to say, and I'm sorry. You were just making headway in that brain of yours—can you please not regress? Pretty please?"*

"I'm not regressing."

"Whatever you want to call it. You should be taking your place as Crone, damn it. You need to—"

A knock sounded simultaneously with the door being thrust open, and Keven eyed me suspiciously from the threshold. "Am I interrupting?"

"Yes," snapped Edie.

"Of course not. I'm just getting dressed."

"I heard voices."

"Voices?" Plural? Had she heard—?

"Your voice," Keven clarified. "Talking to someone." She craned her neck to look behind the door, saw no one, and resumed her narrow-eyed examination of me.

"Just myself," I said, wondering how she and Lucan would

react if they knew about my voices. Thousands of them, according to Edie. But there was only silence in my head now.

Keven grunted. "Well. When you're dressed, the Water Crone would like you to join her for breakfast."

"Oh." My mood brightened at the thought of not having to eat alone again. "Is she feeling—"

The door closed on my question, and Keven's heavy tread continued down the corridor toward the back stairs leading to the kitchen.

"—better?" I yelled the rest of my question after her in a fit of entirely childish pique. I got no response, of course, and so I stuck my tongue out at the door, picked up my pants, and finished dressing. At least Anne wanted to talk to me. It wasn't quite the same as having the old Keven and Lucan back, and I couldn't say I was looking forward to the topic of conversation, but it was better than a kick in the pants, as my grandmother had been fond of saying.

And it was a start.

EXCEPT IT WASN'T AT ALL BETTER THAN A KICK IN THE pants. Not even a little bit.

Not when it turned out that Anne's presence in the dining room came with her protector's, too. Because as much as I wanted to feel sympathy for Bedivere in the face of what Lucan had told me about him being the only protector to lose a Crone, he made it damned difficult. Especially before I'd even had coffee, and he chose the chair directly across the round table from me and fixed me with an unblinking, narrow-eyed stare.

There was a brief moment of respite when Lucan joined us, and my heart did a little dance of joy at not having to face Burly Man and the Water Crone on my own. But Lucan's avoidance of my gaze was as pointed as Bedivere's refusal to look away, and his murmured good morning to Anne but not me dashed any hopes for a champion that I might have harbored. Especially when he chose the chair at Bedivere's side rather than mine.

I scowled to hide my hurt as he tucked into his plate of eggs and sausage. A dozen kicks in the pants would have been infinitely preferable to the one that felt like it had landed square in my belly. What in hell was going on with him? And with Keven, for that matter? I pressed my lips together and clenched my teeth. Whatever it was, I had every intention of finding out after breakfast because I couldn't—wouldn't—go on like this.

Anne pushed the coffee pot toward me with her good arm, and I made an effort to transfer my attention to her. We had things to discuss, too, and judging by her appearance, she was ready. Between her rest and Keven's healing efforts, she was a different woman from the one I'd spoken with on the night of her arrival. Her arm remained splinted, of course, and would still take some time to heal, but apart from that, I would have been hard pressed to recognize her. Her gray-streaked brown hair was neatly braided in two long plaits that hung over her shoulders, her brown eyes fairly sparkled with vigor, and her jaw was set in determination. She wasted no time in getting down to business.

"Right," she said briskly, her words encompassing our entire company—me on one side of the table, Lucan and Bedivere on the other, and Keven stony-faced with folded arms by the door. "We have work to do, starting with finding the others."

She took a mouthful of coffee and froze, her eyes comically wide with shock as several seconds ticked past. Bedivere thrust back his chair, tipping it over onto the floor with a crash.

"Milady!"

Anne set her mug on the table and waved at him, but I wasn't sure if it was in reassurance or a plea for help. Bedivere didn't appear to be certain, either, given how fast he moved to her chair. The Water Crone forced herself to swallow as he crouched beside her in alarm.

"I'm okay," she whispered, her voice hoarse. "Really. I'm fine. Go sit down."

Reluctantly, her shifter did as instructed, and Anne leaned forward to stare into her mug. She raised her gaze to me. "That," she said, shuddering, "is *not* coffee."

"Sadly," I responded, "it is. I've tried to teach her, believe me, but she insists on doing it her way."

"By adding tar?" Anne grimaced.

"She?" Bedivere growled.

"Keven," I answered him first, adding, "the gargoyle," when he continued scowling. The grimace deepened, and I remembered Anne's question on the first night, *"Your gargoyle has a name?"*

I decided the topic was best left alone for the moment and switched my attention back to Anne's question. "She boils it."

"Boils it," Anne repeated. "Boils ... the coffee."

"You get used to it after a while," I promised, but she shook her head and peered again at the mug, this time as if she expected the contents to crawl out of it and come after her. Which, in fairness, they might.

"No," she said. "No, I could survive something like that. Endure it, perhaps. But I could never get used to it." With another shudder, she pushed the mug away. "I'll have tea later. Now. As I was saying, we need to start by locating the others. Bedivere, you'll go back to the Water house and see if you can track—"

"No," growled her protector.

Anne sighed. "I am safe here. I have—"

"I will not leave you, milady." An emphatic shake of Bedivere's head accompanied his second interruption. "Not after what happened, and certainly not with—" He broke off, and his glare—still aimed at me—darkened. "Not with so many unanswered questions."

"Bit of an arrogant prick, isn't he?" Edie observed.

I couldn't very well answer her out loud—at least, not

without lending credence to Bedivere's obvious concerns about me, and so I kept my response to her in my head. *"He's bonded to her as her protector,"* I said, *"he can't leave h—"*

"I'll go," Lucan said, his voice gruff.

My mouth dropped open. Wait—he'd what?

"I've already been scouting the leys leading away from your house, and I think I've found their trail. I was going to speak to you about it this morning."

Wait—he'd *what?*

Anne nodded. "Yes, that might be best. With no bond formed with a Crone for you yet ..." She trailed off and looked at me, as if sensing the hollowness blooming in my chest. The panic rising in my throat.

I knew Lucan had been avoiding me, but he'd been leaving the house? Going elsewhere without me—without even telling me? Did I really mean that little, now that he knew for certain his bond was with another?

"Claire?" Anne reached out to cover my hand with her own. "Are you all right?"

I pulled away from her touch. Heat gathered in my core, feeding my panic. I tried to make it dissipate and couldn't. Fingernails cutting into my palms, I shoved it down and held it there through sheer force of will. I did *not* need to lose it now.

My gaze darted between Anne and Lucan, then landed on Bedivere. I was supposed to start lessons with Anne—and, given the internal war I waged at this very instant, I *needed* lessons—but to remain in the house with Burly Man if Lucan wasn't here? I didn't think so. Bond or no bond, I at least trusted Lucan to intervene if his brother got out of hand.

I wrenched my gaze back to him. "I'll go with you," I said.

All eyes were on me. Lucan shook his head. "Thank you for the offer, milady, but I think it's best if you stay here."

I squared my shoulders and lifted my chin, stubbornness kicking in. I blamed the panic—and Bedivere. "I've defeated the goliath before. If you—"

"No." Lucan's mouth became a tight slash above his beard. "Forgive me, milady, but your powers..."

The fire in my core spread to my cheeks, turning them hot and my mouth dry at his betrayal. It was one thing to share my shortcomings myself, but to have the protector I'd trusted give voice to his mistrust of me? In front of Bedivere, no less? Burly Man would love this, and no doubt add the not-quite accusation to the condemnation he already heaped upon me.

But as damaging as Lucan's words were, I couldn't deny their truth. I would be more hindrance to him than help in his search for the others, and I would most likely end up requiring rescue myself.

The silence in the dining room drew out uncomfortably, and then Anne cleared her throat and attempted to save what little face I had left.

"Lucan is right," she said. "We don't know what we'll face when he finds the others, and we need to prepare ourselves here."

I needed to get a grip, she meant. On my magick and myself.

She was right, too.

But dear goddess, how could I, without Lucan?

CHAPTER 8

AFTER BREAKFAST, ANNE WENT TO LIE DOWN BEFORE HER first attempt to teach me the craft. It was a wise idea, in my opinion, given the amount of energy she would likely expend. Bedivere followed her upstairs, and I went into the front entry, ostensibly to practice with my staff.

My efforts there were lackluster at best, however, and after a few minutes, I admitted defeat to myself and went in search of gargoyle and shifter. If Lucan was leaving today, we needed to clear the air between us first.

I found them both in the kitchen, where Keven was packing a messenger-style bag on the table. They looked up as I marched into the room, carried more by sheer determination than actual courage, but Keven spared me only the briefest of glances before she returned to packing paper-wrapped herbs into the bag, pushing Mergan away as the cat tried to crawl inside.

"This is the heal-all," she said to Lucan. "You'll recognize it by its smell."

I cleared my throat.

Keven continued as if I weren't there. "You'll need a Crone to activate its full powers, of course, but even without magick, it does a fair job."

I shored up the determination that had brought me this far. Then *ahemmed* loudly.

Keven held up another packet. "This one is for the invisible traumas. Both Crones should take it."

I put a hand on the canvas bag, holding it shut against Keven. She fell silent. Lucan stared at a spot beyond my shoulder. I glared at the pair of them, a flush of irritation starting in my core. "Really? It's bad enough that you avoid me, but you're seriously going to ignore me when I'm standing right next to you?"

Keven blinked at me, then exchanged a look with Lucan. "You have to tell her," she said.

"Why do *I* have to tell her?"

"Tell me what?" I asked.

Lucan glowered at the stone-faced gargoyle who stood with arms on haunches, then he sighed. "Fine," he growled. He turned his face to me but didn't quite manage to meet my gaze. "It's just ... honestly, milady, none of us has ever faced a situation quite like this one."

The gargoyle let out a gusty sigh like the wind whistling through a rocky crevice, and Lucan tightened his lips. "What I mean is—"

"For goddess's sake, mutt, get to the point," growled Keven.

Lucan rubbed a hand over his face, palm rasping against his beard, looking like he wanted to be anywhere but here. Anywhere but with me.

"Tell me what?" I asked again.

Keven took over. "You know there have always been just four Crones, and that each of them has had a house with a gargoyle and a protector."

I nodded.

"You're not one of them."

"*Oof,*" said Edie, choosing that moment to join us. "*Not one to pull punches, is she?*"

I ignored her. "Of course I know that," I said, with far more equanimity than I felt. I took my hand away from the bag, and Mergan resumed his efforts to crawl inside. "Which means you and Lucan don't serve me. I get that. But it doesn't explain the cold shoulder since Anne and Bedivere arrived."

"Before *Lady* Anne arrived," Keven said with deliberate emphasis, "we had no other responsibility, because we had no other Crone. And because you are the Fifth, we didn't know if the other pendants had even found their Crones. Now, we do."

I must have looked as confused as I felt, because Lucan cleared his throat.

"You see, milady, the four pendants always choose their Crones at the same time, but we didn't know if your pendant worked in the same manner. If its choosing was connected to the others."

"Until Lady Anne," I said.

"Until Lady Anne," he agreed. "We know now that Fire, Air, and Water have been chosen, which means Earth must have been, too."

"And now that we do know," Keven said, her voice flat, "our loyalty—and Lucan's bond of protection—is to her, not you."

Like Edie said, not one to pull her punches.

I blinked back the prickle behind my eyes and held onto my pride with both hands—that being the only thing that kept me from dissolving into snivels. I made myself smile. Or grimace. Or whatever.

"I understand that," I told Keven, with a jerk of my shoulders that wasn't quite the nonchalant shrug I tried for. "But it still doesn't explain why you're both avoiding me. Unless you're planning to throw me out on my ear?"

"Of course not. You are the Fifth Crone, milady," Lucan said. "You are as welcome here as any other Crone."

Relief flooded through me, making me want to cry for a whole other reason. I could stay. The house might not be mine, but I could at least stay. I blinked faster and dug my fingers into both sides of my ribcage, trying to distract my brain. I let out the breath I'd been holding.

"Good to know," I croaked. Nope. Still not achieving nonchalance. I gave up. "But for goodness' sake, if I'm staying, can't we at least still be friends? No more avoiding one another? I've missed you."

Keven stared at me in genuine astonishment. "Friends?" she echoed. "Milady, we were never meant to be *friends*. We served

56

you as our Crone when we thought that was who you were. And now you are not."

My head jerked back as if she'd slapped me. So. I wasn't to be thrown out physically, but in every other aspect, the abandonment I'd feared would be complete. *Was* complete.

The tiny hope to which I'd clung, the hope for at least companionship in my magickal life—my unwanted magickal life—sputtered out of existence. The hollowness of loss that had been in my chest for days yawned wider, swallowing my heart, my lungs. The heat that had been lying dormant since I'd suppressed it at breakfast flared.

Shit, I thought.

"Claire?" Alarm tinged Edie's voice in my head—with good reason.

Fuck.

The heat spread outward from my core, licking through my limbs like the Fire I knew it to be. *Shit-fuck*, I thought again, with an edge of panic. Mergan pulled his head from the bag and tensed, staring at me as the house cringed. My palms itched, then burned.

"Milady," Lucan said. His voice was deep and resonant, with no sign of the urgency I thought the situation warranted.

No control, I thought. *I still have no—*

Strong, warm hands grasped my shoulders. "You aren't alone," Lucan said, once again demonstrating his ability to know my moods. My thoughts.

But the Fire didn't care.

"You will remain with the house and train with Lady Anne," he continued, "and the gargoyle will continue to see to your needs while I search for the others. *You aren't alone.*"

But I was. In every way that mattered, I was.

I struggled to rein in the heat, to break its hold on me—and my unwilling hold on it. It swirled in me, searching for a path out, demanding release. The house pulled further back from me. It braced itself.

"Breathe, Claire," Edie whispered, her voice faint, distant. *"I'm still here with you, remember? Breathe and—"*

The kitchen door crashed open and Bedivere stood framed in its opening, a scowl on his face and his hand curled into a fist. "What the bloody hell is going on?" he snarled, menace in every line of his body. Menace toward me.

And I was to be left on my own with him, with no protector.

Just like that, the Fire in me had a target.

Mergan bolted.

CHAPTER 9

"LADY CLAIRE, NO!" LUCAN SHOUTED, AND HIS WORDS echoed in my brain even as he morphed into his wolf form and leapt toward Bedivere. Blue flames, wolf, and man tangled together. A howl of pain erupted. The house groaned and trembled. Stone hands swung me off my feet and shook me back to full awareness. Back to control. The flames within me shrank back and cooled. My connection to fire snapped.

Utter stillness fell.

Keven released her hold on me and hurried to the men on the floor. Lucan had returned to human form, but he wasn't moving. Neither was Bedivere. Horror filled me, becoming a bitter bile in my chest, my throat, my mouth. I stared at Lucan's empty clothes at my feet. Dear goddess, what had I done?

The bodies on the floor stirred, one naked, one pissed beyond measure.

The pissed one gained his feet in a single, lithe movement that belied his burly stature and lunged toward me with a roar, shoving at the granite bulk blocking his way. Keven held fast.

"Enough!" a new voice commanded. The tiny part of my mind that still functioned, that hadn't begun an inward collapse under the weight of my actions, saw Anne in the doorway, the frame around her still smoldering, smoke curling up from the scorched wood. I saw her expression—a mix of fury, astonishment, and worry, in equal measure. Lucan climbed slowly to his feet beside her, clinging to the blackened doorframe for support as he swayed.

I willed him to look at me. He didn't.

Anne's mouth moved. Words, I thought. She's saying something. But the rush of blood boiling through my body pounded against my eardrums, drowning her out. Drowning everything out. Everything but my Claire-voice, filled with revulsion. Dismay.

"How could *you?"* it whispered.

I had no answer, and so I did the only thing I could. I bolted for the door to the garden, wrenched it open, and ran. Blindly. Heedlessly. A voice called after me. Lucan?

I ran faster, stumbling, catching myself, trampling pell-mell through herbs and vegetables in my headlong flight away from the house, my reluctant companions—and my magick. Above all, my magick. I ran and ran and—

I hadn't even made it to the woods when a solid wall of chest brought me to an abrupt halt, knocking the wind from my lungs and my feet out from under me. I toppled backward, but strong arms caught me before I could fall. Pulled me close. Held me tight.

"Milady, stop," Lucan said. "You cannot outrun it."

I gasped for air, fighting his hold. "Let. Me. Go!"

He tightened his arms around me and rested his chin on my head, tucking me even closer. "I cannot. Not for your sake, not for ours, not for the world's. Whether any of us see it or not, the Morrigan chose you for a reason, Lady Claire, and you are bound by that choice."

"But it wasn't *my* choice!" I wailed.

"Was it not?" he asked, his voice both gruff and patient. He pulled back enough to look down at me, brushing the hair back from my face with one hand. "When the pendant came to you, did you not choose to follow it? And when you found the gate, to summon the gargoyle? And then to follow her to the house? All of those choices *were* yours, Lady Claire, and yours alone. You could have turned away at any of those points."

Even as I shook my head in denial of his words, one of my hands crept up between us and clutched the pendant. Held it. Claimed it. Because I knew he was right. Knew that as much as I had fought the magick, part of me had wanted it, too. It still did.

"But not like this," my Claire-voice whispered. *"Not when it brings so much destruction with it."*

"You *can* learn to control it," Lucan said, reading my mind again. He rested his forehead against mine. "Stay here with Lady Anne. Let her teach you. You have incredible power, milady. You just need to know how to use it."

"And you?" I asked. With the panic leaving my veins and awareness returning, I had realized the chest I rested against was naked, and I suspected the rest of him was, too. Warm and naked with just the right amount of—

Lucan put me gently away from him as if he'd read that thought, too, and mortification gathered in my throat. He seemed unperturbed, however—and, as usual, not nearly as conscious of his nudity as I was.

"I'll go after the others, like I told Lady Anne," he replied. "The Crones need to be together if they—and *you*—are to raise the magick needed to stand against Morok. And I ..." He trailed off.

"You need to find the Earth Crone," I finished, making myself move past the little knife gleefully slicing my heart to ribbons. Past his nakedness and my hormones. Past the aching sense of loss that had been dogging my steps for days—even before Anne's arrival. "Your Crone."

He nodded. "Yes. I do."

I let the full weight of his words settle into me. Braced myself to bear them. Then nodded my acceptance—no, the lie of my acceptance. Because even though I understood, I was a long, long way from accepting.

But that was my problem, not Lucan's.

"You're all right to travel?" I asked. "I didn't ..."

"I'm fine," he said. "And so is Bedivere, apart from his pride."

I shuddered at the name, remembering all the reasons I didn't want to remain here without Lucan. Without the one person who had cared enough to chase me down. The one being who hadn't deliberately turned away from me.

Lucan sighed. "Milady, you need to understand the nature of the magick that created us—me and the others. It's not something we do; it's what we are. It is everything about us. Our very essence. The gargoyles are stone brought to life. They were never human, they will never *be* human, and they cannot form human connections like the friendship you seek. Do you understand?"

I thought back to my conversation with Keven in the garden, when I'd learned about how Merlin-Morok had turned Arthur's knights into wolves when he realized he was losing the battle against the Morrigan-Morgana. How Morgana had brought the gargoyles to life in response. How Keven still carried with her the guilt of the innocent lives she'd taken, among them Lucan's wife and son. How, to this day, she mourned the loss of her kind in the battle and the subsequent splitting of the world by Morgana.

I wanted to tell Lucan that he was wrong about her—that perhaps it wasn't that she *couldn't* feel things like friendship, but that she didn't let herself, because it hurt too much. But Keven's story wasn't mine to tell, and even if I were right—even if that was her reason for shutting me out—it was small comfort.

"Milady?" Lucan tipped my chin up until I met his gaze. "Do you understand?"

"What about you?" I asked, evading the question because I both did and didn't, and it was ... complicated. "What did magick do to you and the other protectors?"

Lucan looked away. "Choice," he murmured, in a voice so low I had to strain to hear it despite being so close I could feel the heat radiating from his body. "It took away our choice." He released my chin and took a step back. "We should go back to the house."

I hugged myself against the loss of his warmth and looked over my shoulder at the solid stone house on the far side of the garden through which I'd trampled, the flattened basil and broken broccoli marking my path. For the first time in weeks, I found no comfort in the house's presence. I didn't feel safe returning to its walls, and I wasn't sure I could bring myself to face the others after what I had done.

But I had nowhere else to go and, as Lucan had pointed out, I couldn't outrun the magick any more than I could outrun myself. My entire being heavy with dread, I turned and picked my way back between rows of plants.

"I'll have a word with the gargoyle before I leave about seeing to your needs," Lucan said behind me as we reached the door, "and with Bedivere about keeping his distance. And, milady, I want you to promise you'll be careful in my absence. Stay close to the others, especially Lady Anne and the gargoyle. I need to know you'll be safe."

My heart gave a jumpy little flutter, and I caught my breath. He *needed* to know? Wasn't that an odd choice of words? Something someone would say if they—I don't know—*cared*?

"I—I—" I stammered.

"Promise me."

I raised my gaze to the familiar amber one that was about to leave me with no guarantee of return. Whether or not he cared, I did. Too much by far, given our roles. I squared my shoulders in an effort to stand tall and on my own two feet, without the support I'd come to expect from him, protector or not. "I promise," I said.

"Thank you." Lucan twisted the knob and opened the door.

The kitchen was empty when we entered. Lucan closed the door again and dropped the wooden bar into place across it. He started across the room, picking up his clothes and the bag Keven had packed for him on his way, lithe and powerful in all his naked glory.

When he reached the doorway to the hall, he stopped to look back at me one last time, his gaze warm and a little sad. "For what it's worth, milady," he said, "if I did have the power of choice, we would indeed be friends."

CHAPTER 10

IN THE HOURS FOLLOWING LUCAN'S DEPARTURE, I wandered aimlessly from room to room, unable to settle. Anne had gone to lie down in the wake of my kitchen fiasco, and if Lucan had spoken with either Keven or Bedivere before leaving, I couldn't tell. Not with the unrelenting continuation of hostilities.

If anything, Keven was even less friendly now than she had been, actively leaving any room I entered instead of simply waiting for me to do so. I tried to apologize for my loss of control, but she never stayed long enough to listen. Mergan avoided me, too, slinking along the walls and through the shadows in Keven's wake, outright running from me if I managed to come too close. And Bedivere...

Bedivere dogged my every footstep, a shadow among shadows. He didn't say a word, but he didn't have to, because his message could not have been clearer. He didn't want me there. Didn't trust me. Didn't think I belonged.

He was right, of course. I'd proved that in spades when I attacked him, but again ... nowhere else to go. At last, sick to death of my own company but unable to avoid myself the way the others could, I went upstairs and headed down the hall toward my bedchamber.

"You need to get over it, Claire," Edie said. *"What happened, happened. You can't change it, so let it go. Let Anne help you the way you told Lucan you would. Use this time to learn—and prove that Neanderthal wrong."*

"And if I can't?"

"Ever heard that thing about crossing that bridge if we come to it?"

"When," I muttered, reaching my door. "It's *when* we come to it."

"Potato, po-tah-to," my dead friend retorted.

Halfway down the corridor, Bedivere's gaze narrowed in suspicion as he heard me apparently talking to myself. Barely stopping myself from flipping him the bird, I twisted the doorknob and stepped inside. I'd never flipped anyone the bird, but it was rapidly becoming a toss-up as to whether Lucan's brother or my former best friend would be the one to break my lifelong streak.

"I'm serious, Claire."

"And I'm tired," I responded. "I'm going to take a bath."

"You know you can't shut me up, right?"

"You know I can ignore you, right?"

"I'll sing, Claire Emerson," she threatened. *"I swear to the goddess …"*

So it was going to be a matter of who was more stubborn, was it? Fine. I could do stubborn. I stomped into the adjoining bathroom and stuffed the plug into the bathtub, then turned on the hot water.

"Ninety-nine bottles of beer on the wall," Edie warbled.

Dear goddess.

"Ninety-nine bottles of beeeeer!"

I gritted my teeth and took a deep breath.

"If one of those bottles should happen to fall—"

"ON TOP OF SPAGHETTI," I sang at the top of my lungs, because it was my grandson's favorite song and all I could think of right now, "all covered in cheese—"

"There'll be ninety-eight bottles of beer on the wall!"

"I LOST MY POOR MEATBALL—"

"Claire!" Anne's shout broke through the cacophony, and I whirled, mouth still hanging open on "meatball," to find her staring at me in mixed horror and fascination. Keven stood at her shoulder.

"I—" Anne peered around the white-tiled room. "Am I interrupting?"

I snapped my mouth shut. "No," I said, shaking my head. "Not at—no."

She regarded me for another second, then graciously let go of her curiosity. "I'm sorry I was sleeping when you got back, but I still tire easily and wanted to rest before we started on your lessons. Why don't we work outside?"

Where I could do less damage?

"Just apologize and get it over with," Edie said.

I wished I could. But shame tangled with the words I wanted to speak, clogging my throat.

Misunderstanding, Anne offered, "I think we should start today, but we can wait until after your bath, if you'd like."

My—I registered the sound of running water and twisted around to turn off the tap. "It's fine," I said. "I wasn't—it can wait."

"Good," she said, turning to go. "I'll meet you in the clearing in front of the house."

"Are you sure it's safe?" I asked. "The wards ..."

"Yes, I noticed they're down. We'll make that our first task. And Bedivere will be with us."

Which would guarantee her safety and my demise, I thought, because Bedivere would—happily and without any hesitation whatsoever—toss me into the jaws of any monster that attacked. But I pulled the plug from the tub without argument and followed her and Keven from the room.

ANNE TURNED IN A CIRCLE IN THE MIDDLE OF THE clearing, hands on hips, *tsking* under her breath as her gaze traveled the treetops. She made three complete revolutions before she faced me, her expression somber.

"I was wrong," she said. "The wards aren't just down. They're

..."

"Gone," I replied. "I know."

And nothing had been able to coax them back. Not the treats Keven left out for them, not the combined efforts of the midwitches, nothing. Because of me. Because of that night.

The chill October wind slid beneath my shirt, and I shivered, wishing I'd worn my cloak—or a sweater. Wishing I still *owned* a sweater. But all my belongings had gone up in flames with my old house, and while my daughter-in-law had very generously given me her credit card and *carte blanche* for spending, I was lucky to have underwear. I never lasted more than a few minutes in a store before my paranoia became too much and I fled back to the relative safety of the house.

Relative safety, because with no wards, it had been about as protected as any other building in the town of Confluence. Probably less so, considering the wards the midwitches had placed around my son's home and business, and around the house of Jeanne, my neighbor-friend who might still be a target in the Mages' attempt to get at me. But warded or not, the house had been solid and welcoming, and it had been the only home I had left.

Had been.

And wasn't anymore.

"Claire?"

Anne was looking askance at me, and my cheeks warmed. "Sorry. I was ..."

"Out of your depth?" Her brown eyes were sympathetic, and I gritted my teeth against the self-pity piling up in my throat. I stared past her shoulder at the woods, the house looming at my back. Despite the scarred trees standing in silent testimony to the destruction I'd unleashed that night, the forest had repaired a lot of the damage I'd inflicted on it, thanks to the Earth magick that flowed from the house. Keven had told me it was my doing, not the house's, but I suspected she was humoring me in an effort to keep me from giving up altogether. Because after I'd killed the mages, I was nowhere near connected enough to Earth to wield that kind of magick.

Or to Air.

Or to Water.

Or to Fire.

"Anne, am I a mistake?" I blurted. Then I held my breath. As much as I hadn't wanted any of this seven short weeks ago, I suspected Lucan had been right about me choosing it after all. Bit by bit, decision by decision, until I couldn't imagine my life without it. Couldn't really remember what I had been without it —or who.

Until I was terrified by the possibility I might have to return to being that person if I couldn't learn to be the Crone I needed to become.

I looked at Anne, who hadn't answered. She regarded me pensively, cradling her injured arm in her good one, her long, gray-streaked hair lifting around her shoulders in the breeze. Looking every inch the wise woman of power that I wasn't.

"I don't know," she said at last.

It wasn't the answer I'd hoped for.

"There's never been a Fifth Crone before," Anne continued. "None of us knew when one would arrive, or what she would be like. Only the Morrigan could tell you that."

My brain dredged up a memory made hazy by the fever and infection that had raged through my body at the time, thanks to the gnome bite on the back of my leg. A woman, half-crow and half-human—or had she just been dressed in crows? I couldn't grasp the image, only the impression. But I remembered the drink she'd offered me: the dark, foul liquid that stank of rot and death. I remembered how I'd gagged and thrust it away, and her words to me when I did.

"You'll do. That was the Cup of Power. If you had been tempted by it, I would have let the infection take you here and now. But you weren't, and so I will save you that you may serve me."

She'd said she was the Morrigan, but I'd never quite believed she hadn't been just a hallucination. And even if she'd been real, the vague sense of shame over her less-than-ringing endorsement of *"you'll do"* would have kept me from sharing the experience with either Keven or Lucan. But maybe Anne—

"And since the goddess hasn't revealed herself to any of us since she merged with Morgana, it's not like we can ask," Anne added. "So I say we work on the assumption that you're exactly who you're supposed to be and see about teaching you some of those magick skills you need."

—or maybe not.

Perhaps if I'd managed to connect to all the elements in the weeks since the attack—if I'd shown any aptitude or a hint of promise—perhaps, then, I might have told her. But imposter that I was already convinced I might be, I wasn't keen to announce that I, the unknown quantity in this Crone scenario, was the first and only one to have seen the Morrigan since Morgana herself. Not yet. Not until I could prove—even if only to myself—that the Morrigan would have had reason to show herself to me. To choose me at all.

"Tell me what happened in the kitchen earlier," she said, "when you summoned Fire."

"When I almost burned the house down again, you mean?"

"I'm guessing it wasn't on purpose."

"Hardly. I was just ..." I trailed off, unwilling to admit I'd been afraid—no, terrified—at the thought of being alone, without Keven and Lucan to look out for me. That the terror had coalesced at my core, and Keven's denial of friendship had been like a catalyst. That my sense of abandonment had become a fire I couldn't hold onto, couldn't control.

And then Bedivere had come into the room, and—

My breath caught.

Wait. Could that be it? Could it really be that simple? That obvious? My gaze swiveled back to the Water Crone.

"I've been *upset*," I said.

Her brows drew together. "I'm ... sorry? Was it something I

69

said?"

I uncrossed my arms to wave away her confused apology. "No. I mean, I was—emotional. Every time I've connected with one of the elements, I've been emotional about something. When the shade attacked my house, it was fear." I held up one hand, thumb outstretched as a marker. "When I threw the table at Keven and rooted myself to the floor, anger." My index finger joined the thumb. "When I caused the storm, frustration." My middle finger. "And when—"

"Wait—you rooted yourself to the floor?" Anne broke in.

I flapped my hand with the extended digits at her. "I told you about that."

"I think I would have remembered if you had."

"Whatever. The point is, every time it's happened, I've been feeling super intense about something. That helps, right? It gives us somewhere to start?" Hope made me lightheaded, and I wanted to dance a little jig on the spot.

But Anne was biting her bottom lip and shaking her head. Doubt clouded her expression. "I'm sorry, but I don't think so. Magickal connections don't work that way. They're deliberate. Purposeful. Magick itself is about intention. I'm not sure why the connections are happening for you otherwise, but that's not how you'll learn to control them."

My fingers and thumb curled back into my palm, and my shoulders slumped. Of course it wasn't. Because goddess forbid anything about this would make even the slightest bit of sense or be even the slightest bit easy.

"*It's complicated,*" I'd told Bedivere when he'd been asking his questions on that first night.

He didn't know the half of it.

Sensing my mood's nosedive, Anne came over and nudged my ribs with her good elbow. "Come on," she said, "We'll start by calling the wards back. It's one of the simplest things I can think of to master. It will give you a confidence boost."

If only, I thought, as I trailed her toward the trees.

CHAPTER 11

THE LESSON WENT ABOUT AS I EXPECTED, LEAVING ANNE frustrated and me resigned. She started by showing me how to cast a circle—a simple enough operation that involved invoking each of the elements at their associated compass points as I walked in a circle around her: Earth to the north; Fire to the south; Air to the east; and Water to the west.

Circles functioned as spots of magickal intention, she explained. They helped to focus the spell-caster, and they also provided protection once raised, because they attracted wards to them.

Mine did not.

We waited for a while, then Anne had me recast the circle. Then we moved to a different location. Then Anne cast the circle herself. Then we moved again. The sun dipped behind the trees, and dusk claimed the clearing. We waited some more.

Nothing.

No sparks of light that looked like fireflies. No net of energy stretched above us. No hint of any lives other than our own.

"I've never seen anything like it," Anne murmured, doing yet another revolution in the center of my last effort. Her good hand rested on her hip, and she shook her head, looking tired and in need of rest again.

I cast a surreptitious glance toward Bedivere, who hovered just inside the tree line, expecting to find him glaring at me. He didn't disappoint.

"Not ever," Anne continued. "I mean, even a raw novice with no craft experience at all can still call at least a *few* wards."

I grimaced. So much for that boost of confidence she'd promised me. Catching sight of my face, Anne forced a not particularly convincing smile.

"Never mind," she said. "I'm sure they'll come back."

Eventually.

The unspoken word hung like a dark cloud over the circle I'd made, raising all sorts of silent questions. Would they return in time? Or would the Mages track Anne here and attack again before they did?

I shook off the day's failures—at least I was getting good at that part—and used my right hand to cut an imaginary line through the circle I'd raised. Not that I would have walked into a wall of wards if I hadn't broken the circle that way—because again, no trace of those—but because Anne had said it was a good habit to get into, regardless.

Just in case she was right, and they did return. Eventually.

"We should go in," I said. "It's getting dark."

Off in the trees, a twig snapped, underscoring my suggestion —and the reason behind it. If something came out of the woods, Bedivere would be there to protect her. I was on my own.

"... promise me you'll be careful in my absence ... I need to know you'll be safe."

"You're right," Anne agreed, not quite hiding her sigh. "We'll try again tomorrow."

She headed toward the house, Bedivere following a few feet behind and to her left. I started after them, but halfway across the grassy clearing, my steps slowed and stopped. I gazed back toward the woods and the path I'd trodden through them when I'd first discovered the house. I'd traveled it several times since, as I'd moved back and forth between lives, before my old one had been irrevocably torn from me with the death of Edie and the loss of my home. But now a sudden longing seized me. I thought of the street I'd lived on for thirty years, the neighbors I'd chatted with, the garden I'd tended, the friends I'd made, and oh, goddess, how I missed them. I ached with missing them.

Even Jeanne, my across-the-street neighbor whose friendship had been my ex-husband's idea rather than my own.

Even my ex-husband.

"Now you're pushing it," Edie muttered.

I sniffled and swiped a hand over my cheek. "I'm just ..."

Edie sighed. *"I know, hon. I know."*

And, dear goddess, I wished I could hug my irascible friend herself, no matter how nuts she made me sometimes.

"I know that, too," Edie said. *"But we'll get through this. Together, because I'm right here with you. I promise."*

"Claire?" Anne's voice called through the gathering dark.

I turned from the woods. "Coming," I replied, and I started toward the figure framed in the light spilling from the house.

Perhaps Edie followed me. Perhaps she didn't.

Because, despite her promise, I had no way of telling.

DINNER WAS A SILENT AFFAIR, EATEN BY THE FOUR OF US— Anne, Bedivere, Keven, and me—in the kitchen together but not really shared. Keven had set three places in the dining room, but I'd arrived there first, taken one look, then collected my dishes and carried them to the worn kitchen table to join the gargoyle. I couldn't face eating across the dining room table from Bedivere, and I thought Keven's company, no matter how silent, would be preferable. Her judgment of me more manageable.

But as soon as I sat down, Anne arrived, too, with Bedivere carrying both their place settings. He all but slammed the dishes onto the table before taking the seat across from me, and then I faced the judgment of not just one, but all three. And the silence. Oh, the silence. Thick and heavy, it sat over the room like a stifling wool blanket. My stomach churned.

Keven set bowls in the center of the table, each landing with a distinct thump. Freshly baked rolls, roasted carrots, mashed potatoes, thick slabs of roasted venison swimming in gravy. She and Bedivere heaped their plates, Anne to a lesser degree, and I, even less. Then I pushed what little food I had taken around my plate, arranging and rearranging potatoes in one pile, carrots in another, chunks of meat in a third, and making trails with my fork tines through the thick gravy connecting them. But I didn't eat. How could I, with Keven refusing to look at me and Bedivere refusing to look away?

Anne seemed the only one unaware of anything amiss, calmly scooping bites into her mouth and chewing, pausing to compliment Keven's cooking, breaking off bits of bread roll to mop up her own gravy. Goddess, how I envied her poise and confidence. I, meanwhile, felt increasingly inept in her presence. How on earth would I survive when I had to face all four of the Crones together?

Abruptly, I pushed my plate away and stood. Anne looked up at me, Bedivere never once looked elsewhere, and Keven continued staring at her plate and chewing methodically. I'd had all I could handle for one day.

"I think I'll go take that bath," I said.

"You haven't eaten." Anne frowned. "Are you all right?"

Asked the injured woman of the whole one.

I swallowed a surge of self-pity—and the tears that threatened to accompany it. I was damned if I'd cry in front of Bedivere. Or Keven, for that matter.

"I'm just tired," I said. "It's been a long day." My mouth twisted. Right. A long day of accomplishing nothing—again. Unless I counted trying to kill Bedivere.

But I'd failed at that, too, so—

"*Ouch,*" said Edie. "*You should probably leave before you let that one slip. Just sayin'.*"

Bedivere's dark glower assured me he'd already guessed my thoughts, but I decided to heed Edie's advice before I made matters any worse. I wrenched my gaze away from Bedivere and made myself smile at Anne. "I'll see you at breakfast," I said.

"Of course. Here in the kitchen? I never thought to ask where you preferred to eat. I'm sorry for that."

Keven's head remained steadfastly bent over her plate. Whatever her feelings toward me might be, they were seemingly set in the same stone from which she was carved.

"Honestly?" I said, rather proud of myself for not choking on the word. "I don't think it matters. Wherever you prefer is fine."

With her *sleep well* following me, I left the kitchen and pulled open the barely visible door in the wall that led to the back stairs. I climbed them wearily, wondering where Lucan was right now and how long it would take him to track the others through the ley lines. When he would return with them. What my life would hold when they arrived.

I reached the second floor and started down the corridor to my door. A single sconce came on halfway down the hall, providing just enough light for me to travel without colliding with the wall. Once, the sconces lining the walls had come on one at a time, lighting my way as I went, but apparently Crone houses, like gargoyles and shifters, could hold grudges.

I pushed open my bedchamber door, stepped halfway into the darkened room, and then froze as something rustled in the shadows. I inhaled a raw, ragged breath as a figure loomed beside the bed, and in the tiny space between heartbeats, a hundred thoughts collided at once in my brain. Lucan had returned—no, the Mages had found us—they'd sent another monster—a shade —and I had no staff with me—*run!*

The last thought exploded through my entire being as the figure flew apart. A rush of wings filled the air, coming straight at me, and I staggered backward, tripping and sprawling onto the hall floor. My cry tangled with the beat of wings against my head. I fought them off with both hands, thrusting them away even as the sound of footsteps pounding up the stairs penetrated.

Even as a cooler, calmer part of my mind finally, belatedly recognized the wings for what they were—and what they were not.

Crows, not a shade.

Crows that had formed a gown covering a woman I had seen

before. A woman I'd thought I had dreamed. A woman who had dissolved before my eyes as the crow gown came apart when I opened the door. A woman who had hissed a message at me that I had almost missed amid the thunderous flapping of wings and my own scream.

The rush of wings faded, disappearing as the footsteps burst into the corridor behind me. Keven arrived first. She stood without offering help, scowling from me to the open door of my room and back. Anne and Bedivere's wolf were next, she crouching next to me and he beside her, bristling and poised for attack.

"Claire, what is it? What happened?" Anne pushed my hair out of my face and ran her good hand over my arms and legs, searching for injury, her eyes anxious. "Are you hurt?"

"Crows," I said. I looked past Anne at the empty room beyond. "I saw the crows again."

It was on the tip of my tongue to tell her about the woman, too—about the gown that had come apart into a murder of crows, and the hissed warning—but I held back. Now was not the time. Not with Bedivere and Keven here.

My gaze found and settled on the gargoyle in the corridor. I'd hesitated to tell her for too long, and now, with her new disinterest in what happened to me, I wasn't sure I trusted her to believe me.

My breath hitched a little at the thought, but I shrugged it off. I was still far too near tears—or more serious upset—to want to analyze the realization too closely. It would be like playing with Fire, so to speak.

As for Bedivere—I turned my gaze to the shifter, who had morphed back into human form and was standing with hand and stump resting on naked hips, his jaw clenched against words I suspected would be both angry and directed at me.

Him, I didn't trust at all.

So I stayed quiet and endured the fussing while Anne sent Keven for tea and oversaw the running of my bath. I watched her summon bubbles to the water, smiled my thanks, and heard the Morrigan's warning over and over again in my head as I tried to stay present and coherent.

Fifteen minutes later, with a last few clucks of concern over me, the Water Crone finally left, taking Bedivere and Keven with her. I waited until the door clicked shut behind them, and then began undressing as I stared at my reflection in the mirror. Goddess, but I looked exhausted. Every single one of my sixty years was carved into my wan face, and—

"Beware!" the Morrigan hissed again in my head. I flinched and spun around to face the empty room.

Beware. Beware what? And how in all of creation could I possibly be any more *ware*? I already jumped at shadows and sounds—and sometimes at nothing at all. I expected disaster at every turn. I'd learned what it was like to sleep with one eye open. I—

A knock sounded at the door, making me start and proving my point. Grimacing at my shaking fingers, I buttoned my shirt again. I knew the Morrigan had intended to warn me, but by the goddess herself, couldn't she have been more helpful about it? The knock at the door came again—more of a pounding, really—and I bit back a groan. That sounded ominously *not* like a woman's summons, and it lacked the hollow boom of Keven's granite fist against wood, which left ...

I twisted the knob and took a hasty step back as Bedivere grabbed the door's edge and thrust his way into the room. He might not have been as tall as his brother, but he was just as imposing, and his presence dominated both doorframe and room. At least he was dressed again—thank the goddess for small mercies.

I tried not to shrink away as he advanced and stood over me. He wasted no time in going on the attack.

"I don't know what game you're playing," he snarled, "but it won't fly with me. I saw no crows. I heard no crows. *No one* saw or heard them, *milady.*"

I flinched at the derisive emphasis placed on the title.

Belvidere bouldered on. "I'm watching you. Every minute of every day, *I am watching you.* And if you make a single move toward Lady Anne, I will *end* you. Are we clear?"

"If this is about what happened in the kitchen—" I began, hating the wobble in my voice.

"This is about *you.*" He poked a finger into my breastbone, hard enough to make me stagger back a step. "All of you. Everything about you."

"Damn it, Bedivere, I'm not your enemy." I drew myself up, trying to look stronger than I felt. It had been a bitch of a day—a bitch of a week—hell, it had been a bitch of several weeks, and goddess knew I was trying. But every new revelation, every new thing that happened, was beginning to feel like sandpaper being dragged over raw skin. Right now, all I wanted was to crawl into the tub, let the water close over my head, and block out the world, even for a few seconds.

Or maybe I could just cry.

That was a distinct possibility, too.

Bedivere, however, would not be sympathetic to my tears, so I firmed up my backbone (and my resolve) and added, "I may not be what you expected—what any of us expected—but I am still Crone."

He stepped forward, his face close enough that I could see the pores of his skin and smell the remains of dinner on his breath.

"You," he sneered, "are nowhere near Crone, and your wishful thinking and flimsy grasp on magick will serve no purpose but to endanger the ones who are. So, I repeat, the slightest hint that you're a threat to Lady Anne, and I will end you. *Now* are we clear?"

Apparently we were, because, without waiting for my answer, he spun on his heel and stalked out the door. I stared at the emptiness he left behind for long, long seconds before I convinced my body to move forward and my hand to reach out and close the door. I didn't need to look down the corridor to know that the shifter had morphed into wolf form and taken up his position outside Anne's door. Or that he still stared in my direction. I could feel the raw energy boiling off him and rolling down the hall toward me. The malevolence.

I leaned against the door and squeezed my eyes shut, shuddering in the aftermath of his anger. His hatred. I knew he was driven by his bond to the Water Crone and that he was only acting in what he thought to be her best interests, but dear goddess, was I really that threatening? Could I not catch a single break?

"Edie?" I whispered to the empty room. But despite her assurances that she would remain with me, no answer came. I blinked back the tears that seemed omnipresent these days. With all my heart, I wished again that I could have one last hug from my friend. Edie had always given the fiercest, most bolstering hugs I had ever known, and goddess knew I could use a little bolstering right now. And a little ferocity.

And a friend.

Leaving the bath to go cold, I crawled under my duvet, still fully clothed.

CHAPTER 12

"How are you today?" Anne asked, her manner solicitous at breakfast the next morning as she poured me a cup of tea. "Did you sleep all right?"

I would have preferred the coffee I usually had in the morning, but despite Keven's manner toward me of late, I still wanted to trust her. Wanted to believe that, if she'd hadn't made coffee for me, it would be because the tea contained something I needed. Courage, perhaps. Or wisdom.

"Perhaps the wisdom to leave," my Claire-voice suggested darkly.

I ignored her and murmured my thanks to Anne for the tea. She took her place across from me at the dining room table, and I added, "And I'm fine. Thank you for asking."

Especially since Bedivere wasn't with us.

Brown eyes, too astute for comfort, regarded me across the table. Anne passed me a plate of toast—heavily buttered, the way I liked it. Gone were the days when I allowed myself only the thinnest scraping of vegan margarine. I liked butter, and I really didn't give two figs what it did to my waistline.

I helped myself to two slices.

"Did you sleep?"

I held back a snort and offered a lie instead. "I managed."

"Lucky you." She sighed. "That's the one thing that's eluded me since I hit perimenopause. Fifteen years now without a decent night. If you ask me, it's highly unfair. First, periods; then pregnancy; then childbirth and nursing; then perimenopause; then menopause. I swear, if men had to do all that, there'd be a great deal more research into how to make all of it more comfortable."

My lips tilted upward as I took a sausage and some scrambled eggs from a platter. "Either that or humankind would have gone extinct by now."

Anne chuckled, and she raised her teacup in a salute. "Amen to that, sister." Then she got down to business. "So. The crows last night. How many?"

My appetite evaporated. Crap. Couldn't I have had breakfast first? I pushed my eggs around the plate.

"Too many to count," I said. "And they weren't ..."

"Weren't what?"

"They weren't ordinary crows." That was part of what had kept me awake half the night. And with no Bedivere present, now was the time to tell her. "Not like the ones I usually see, I mean. They were ... they were a gown. On the Morrigan."

Anne went still, toast poised for a bite. "How do you know that's who it was?"

"I've seen her before. Talked with her. After the gnome bit me."

"You didn't tell me about that. Or about a gnome."

"It happened after my house burned down. My real ... my old ... the house I lived in before I found this one. Lucan and I were on the way back from the fire when the gnomes attacked. One of them bit me, and—"

"Gnomes," she said.

"Garden ones. You know, the ceramic kind."

One of Anne's eyebrows lifted so high that I was pretty sure it caused a half-dozen new lines on her forehead. I sighed, backtracked, and told her the full story about the hundreds of ceramic gnomes that had come to life and formed a gauntlet along the path to the house; how I'd used poor Mergan in his carrier as a battering ram; how I'd almost made it to safety when one of the gnomes had sunk its teeth into the back of my thigh; how I'd fallen into fevered unconsciousness and seen the Morrigan.

How I'd conversed with her and spurned the Cup of Power she'd offered me.

How she had said that I would do.

I skipped the part where I'd sung Love Potion Number 9 to Lucan in my semi-conscious state, however. Some things were meant to be kept between a Crone and her not-protector, if only so the Crone didn't have to leave the country.

"I see," said Anne when I'd finished. "And you never told Keven or Lucan about your vision?"

"I thought I'd dreamed it." I gave up all pretense of eating and set aside my fork. "That I was hallucinating because of the fever. But then, last night ... last night, I saw her again. The same figure, the same robe made of crows. It was only for a second, but I'm certain it wasn't a dream."

"And did she say anything?"

"*Beware*," I said. "That was it. Nothing more. I don't—"

Anne surged to her feet.

✦

"But, milady—" Bedivere trotted after Anne like a well-trained puppy as she strode down the corridor from the dining room toward the front of the house. I trailed them both, keeping my distance from the shifter.

Anne cut him off. "No buts. When the Morrigan herself tells us to beware, we *beware*. You are to find Lucan and bring him back here, whether or not he has located the others. I don't care if you have to hog-tie him to do so."

Bedivere slanted me a filthy look that promised I would pay for what he obviously considered my lie to Anne. He returned to his argument with her. "I cannot leave you—"

"You can and you will, because I am ordering you to."

"I won't," he countered, "because I am bound by something greater than you to remain at your side."

They'd reached the front entry hall and stood toe-to-toe, each glaring at the other, neither backing down. Even if I'd been a betting woman, I wouldn't have been willing to put my money on either of them, because from what I'd seen of each of them, it seemed likely the standoff would last forever.

But just as I was weighing the wisdom of intervening, a knock sounded at the door, and Anne and I both froze as Bedivere morphed into his wolf form and his clothes settled in a heap on the floor. Anne kicked them aside and looked at me.

"Are we expecting someone?" she murmured.

I shook my head, cold clawing its way up my spine with needle-like fingers. "No one," I whispered back. In the aftermath of my vision of the Morrigan and her warning, an unexpected visitor didn't bode well, especially since no one was supposed to be able to find the house in the first place. No one except a Crone, that was. And a Crone wouldn't knock.

Keven strode into the hall, wiping her hands on the pinafore I'd made. "It's Kate," she told me. "I saw her from the garden."

I sagged a little, but my relief didn't last. A midwitch wouldn't be coming for tea and biscuits. Something was wrong. The Morrigan's whisper rose again in my mind. *"Beware!"*

"Kate?" asked Anne.

"A local midwitch," Keven said, shoving the growling Bedivere away from the door with one foot. "She assisted us in the attack."

"And she's been looking after my family," I added, wedging myself between Keven and the door to yank on the handle. A startled Kate Abraham, her hand raised to knock a second time, almost fell over the threshold.

I didn't bother with a greeting—or with a fully formed question. "Paul?" I demanded. "Braden? Natalie?"

"All fine," she said, tugging the bulletproof vest of her police uniform into place. "But we have activity." Her gaze went past me to Anne, then dropped to the bristling wolf at Anne's side. She frowned. "That's not Lucan."

"We've had activity, too," I said. I stepped back and waved her into the entry. "Kate, this is Anne, the Water Crone, and her protector, Bed—"

Her sharp eyes swung back to me. "Where's Lucan?"

"He's gone to find the oth—"

"He *left* you?" Kate planted hands on the wide gun belt swallowing her hips and gaped at me. "He can't do that—he's your protector."

I swallowed hard against the sting of her words. "It's a long story," I said, even though it wasn't really. I just didn't want to have to explain something that still felt so raw. So personal. And I *did* want to know what had brought Kate to the house. I waved an impatient hand. "You said we had activity. What kind?"

Kate looked like she might pursue the topic of Lucan, but then she gave an impatient, *whatever* kind of sigh and said, "Mages. Twenty of them so far. They've set up in groups of five at the four points."

"Beware!" hissed the memory of the Morrigan in my brain, and I flinched as a murder of crows exploded toward me in my mind's eye. Anne caught her breath and stared at me. Keven grunted. Bedivere morphed back into naked human form, and Kate stared at him. Dear goddess, but he was one hirsute man, I turned my back on him.

"Twenty?" I echoed. "You're sure?"

That was a lot of Mages. Far, far more than the three I'd had to defeat.

"In groups of five," Kate repeated. "At the four points."

I'd heard her the first time, but her grim emphasis gave me the feeling I was missing something. I looked askance between her and Anne, who looked equally grim.

"You'd better come in," she told Kate. "Gargoyle, we'll take our tea in the sitting room. Bring an extra cup for Kate."

OVER TEA, KATE RELATED THE MIDWITCHES' DISCOVERY OF Mage presence in town. The first sign, she told us, had been the

uneasiness among the wards she and the other midwitches had
set up around town.

"They're still holding," she assured Anne, "but they're rest-
less. Especially where the groups have gathered."

"I imagine they are," Anne murmured.

"What about the ones you set up at Paul's house?" I asked.
"They're still in place, too?"

She nodded. "So far, yes. We've had midwitches keeping an
eye on their house—and on your old neighbor's, too, just in
case. We haven't seen any sign of Mages at either place. From
what we can tell, they're just sitting at the four corners. Like
they're waiting for something."

I shivered and clutched the mug of rapidly cooling tea
against me. I hadn't even tasted it yet because I didn't trust
myself to be able to swallow through a throat thickened by foreboding—and now, by remembered terror.

Braden.

My grandson's screams from the night the goliath took him
had never stopped reverberating in my skull. I heard them in my
dreams and in my unguarded awake moments. He and his
parents might not remember, thanks to the potion and new
memories Keven and Kate had instilled in them, but I? I would
never forget.

And I still couldn't protect them.

Kate leaned forward, resting her elbows on knees spread
wide and letting her linked hands drop between.

"What do you want us to do?" she asked, directing the question, I noticed, to Anne. "I can put out a call, see if I can round
up some extra hands?"

Anne turned her head to stare into the fire, tapping a finger
against her lips. "Groups of five," she murmured. "I don't like
that at all."

"It's worrisome," Kate agreed, running a hand over her short-
cropped hair. It had changed since the last time I'd seen her,
turning from salt-and-pepper to all salt. Probably from sheer

stress. "But not unmanageable, if we have enough of us in town."

"Hm," said Anne. "But five at each of the corners says they're planning something you might not be able to handle on your own. And I'm not much help right now." She held up her splinted arm. "Even if I wasn't injured, there's only one of"—her gaze flicked to me—"two of us. If they summon the goliath again, that won't be enough."

Kate snorted. "I've seen Claire in action," she said grimly. "If she calls on the elements again the way she did that night, she can take out the goliath, the Mages, and most of the town."

"And that," Anne said quietly, "is a whole other problem."

Ouch.

I mean, she was right, but still ... ouch. I took a mouthful of cold tea and choked it down. Silence settled between my companions, and I cleared my throat and used the opportunity to ask a question that had been nagging at me since Kate's arrival. "You keep going back to the groups of five idea. Why is that significant?"

"Chaos," Kate said. "Five is the number of chaos."

That didn't sound good, I thought. Then something occurred to me, and I frowned at her over my teacup. "Wait. There are five of us, too, aren't there? Because I'm the Fifth—"

I stopped as Kate's gaze shifted away to meet Anne's across the wooden chest between the sofas. The proverbial penny dropped.

Ah.

"And double-ouch," murmured Edie.

I scowled. *Not helping, Edie. And if the only reason you're going to turn up is to rub salt into the wound, could you not?*

"Five is more than pure chaos," Anne hastened to reassure me. "In numerology, it can also be the number of the unconventional. Someone who doesn't follow the crowd and does things their own way."

Someone like me, who couldn't learn magick to save her own

life, but could take out—as Kate had said—half the town without trying when she did manage to connect. Which pretty much amounted to chaos, when you thought about it.

I set my cold tea on the chest. "So what *do* we do?" I asked Anne.

"I have no idea. All of this is as new to me as it is to you."

I snorted. "Maybe not quite."

She smiled in return, a little gently. A little sadly. A lot concernedly. "Perhaps not," she agreed.

Kate leaned back on the sofa and linked her fingers behind her head, one ankle resting on the opposite knee. "We need a plan," she said. "I say we throw all ideas on the table and start there."

"I like the idea of calling in more help," Anne said. "It certainly can't hurt. How many witches are here now? And how many more can you find?"

"There are four midwitches in town at the moment, and two within an hour's drive. I'm not sure how many lesser witches—many are solitaries who have been here longer than I have. Confluence seems to attract those who practice the craft."

"Confluence?" Anne asked. "Is that the name of the town?"

Kate and I both nodded, and Anne looked as if a light bulb had gone off in her brain. "I know where I am," she said. "Confluence, Ontario."

"Umm..." I said, and she flapped her good hand at me.

"Ley lines don't come with a map. When you travel them, you have no idea where you'll end up. I hadn't thought to ask you, but I know this place—or at least of it—and oh, this is marvelous. We can use this."

She uncurled herself from the sofa and began pacing the room. Her limp, I noted, was improving. "This area was once a sacred meeting place for the Algonquin. There are three rivers that come together and form a waterfall just north of town, correct?"

Kate nodded. "We rescue several people a year from the thing—or from the caves behind it."

"A confluence," Anne said. "A meeting of three rivers, and a place of power that connects us to land, water, and sky. We can *use* this." She stopped beside the fireplace and whirled to face us. "Is the sense of that power what drew both of you here?"

"Luck of the draw for me. I was assigned by the force—the Ontario Provincial Police." Kate said with a shrug. She sent me a sideways look of question.

"I—" About to say *moved here because of my husband*, I stopped, thinking back more than thirty years. To a time when Jeff had cared at least a little for my opinion and had settled on Confluence to set up his business because I had fallen in love with the little town. Of course, my input had ended there, but still ... what *had* brought me here? "I don't know," I said slowly. "I just felt like I ... belonged."

"So that's a yes, then," said Kate.

Prickles slithered down my spine. Could I really have been drawn here by a power I didn't even know about thirty years ago? Had the Morrigan already singled me out as the Fifth Crone?

Anne was pacing again, nodding with each step. "We have to assume the Mages are aware of its power as well, and that they're here because of it. Most likely to harness it, but why?" She stopped by the window and stared outside for a few seconds. Kate and I both waited. Anne sighed and turned back to us, her lips set, her broken arm held close. "We need to be ready for whatever they might throw at us, so yes, Kate, call whoever can come. We'll set up groups of five ourselves, to counter theirs. Make sure there's at least one midwitch in each, and then we'll decide what to do next."

"But what if—" Kate hesitated.

"All ideas on the table, remember?" Anne prompted.

"It's just—the last time the Mages were here, it was for Claire's pendant. Then they went after you and the other

Crones. It stands to reason that they're here for one of you again now, and—" The midwitch police officer broke off and slanted me a tight, half-smile of apology. "Sorry, Claire, but you seem like the most obvious one. The most vulnerable. Not because of your magick, because I'm pretty sure you gave them pause when you defeated that mountain of a monster, but—"

"My family," I finished, because Paul and Natalie and Braden had been sitting at the edge of my consciousness throughout the conversation—for exactly the reason Kate raised now. "You think they make me vulnerable."

"If the Mages go after them again, yes. They do." She assumed I might turn over my pendant in exchange for my family's safety. She might not be wrong.

"But the wards—"

"Again, enough to warn us of Mage presence, but not enough to withstand a direct attack. And we don't have enough midwitches to be everywhere at all times, especially if we're putting one in each group, like Anne said."

"What are you suggesting?"

"A safe house," she said. "This one."

CHAPTER 13

"No," I growled as I stalked down the hall toward the kitchen. "Absolutely not."

"Just hear me out, will you?" Kate trailed after me, her duty boots thudding hollowly against the flagstones in my wake. "The Mages aren't going to risk coming at you directly, not after what happened to their—"

I stopped mid-corridor and whirled to face her. "Their what? Dead companions? Just say it, Kate. I killed three people."

She scowled back at me, hands again resting on her gun belt. "Yes. And if you hadn't, none of us would be here now, discussing our current situation. Hell, none of us would be here, period. Killing those three gave the rest of them a new respect for you. Or at least made you an unknown quantity. We can use that to our advantage."

"I am not endangering my family because of some weak theory."

"It's not a theory, damn it. It's fact. Or, at least, as close to fact as we can get without a lot more information." Kate again raked a hand through her white hair, leaving it standing upright in odd tufts. "Think about it, Claire. If the Mages weren't afraid of you, don't you think they'd have come at you again? And one hell of a lot sooner than now, too? But no. They've had to regroup. Plan. Come up with another way to get at you. As I see it, that way is still your family."

I crossed my arms. "Then why haven't they gone after them already? Why are they waiting?"

"We don't know. But the longer we wait, the more chances they have to act. Do you really want to give them that?"

"And what if it's a trap?" I countered. "Think about it, Kate. There are no wards around the house, I can't access my magick

90

to save my own life, let alone someone else's, and the only protector in the house won't lift a finger to protect anyone but his Crone. If you're wrong about the Mages being wary of me—"

"And if *you're* wrong?" she cut in.

I snapped my mouth shut and glared at her.

"I do believe this is what's called an impasse," said Edie.

The words *oh, fuck off* desperately wanted to escape my throat, but I didn't want Kate thinking they were aimed at her. Even if I rather wanted her to fuck off right now, too.

Kate sighed. "Claire, I know you're scared for them. I get that. But wards aren't enough, and the midwitches can't watch them around the clock. Not when we're going to need all hands on deck to counter the Mage groups. Like it or not, this house is the only place that's withstood an attack so far—because of *you* —and that makes it the safest place your family can possibly be right now."

"She's right," Anne said.

She'd followed us and stood behind Kate, the ever-scowling Bedivere just behind her. Did he even have any other expression? I scowled back, not caring about the potential consequences, wondering if I was right about my magick being tied to my emotional state. I rather hoped it was, because I would like nothing better than to wipe that damned superior look right off his face—for good.

"Down, girl," Edie cautioned.

Anne was still talking. "The Mages won't hesitate to attack a warded house once they're ready, but you have a reputation now, and they might think twice about coming here again. Plus, there are two of us. Between us—"

"No. There's one of us," I corrected, "because we all know how damned useless I am. You've seen for yourself. Whatever it was I called on that night, I've come nowhere near getting a handle on it again."

Anne did me the courtesy of not arguing. She simply raised

the shoulder of her uninjured arm in a lopsided shrug and said, "You're right. I have seen. But the Mages haven't."

And so we came full circle again. I pressed my lips together, dug my fingers into my ribs, and slowly deflated. I wasn't going to win this, especially if Kate was serious about withdrawing the midwitches from Paul's house. My throat tight with fear, I nodded slow acceptance.

"All right," I whispered. "How?"

Kate scuffed the toe of one boot against the flagstone floor. "About that," she said with a grimace. "I'm going to need Keven's help with some potions ... and with carrying your son and his wife in from the car."

A N   H O U R   L A T E R ,   I   S T I L L   H A D N ' T   R E C O V E R E D   F R O M   T H E shock.

"I still can't believe you drugged my family and brought them here without even consulting me. How in *hell* am I supposed to explain—" I glared at Kate as I waved both my hands at the corridor, Keven, Anne, Bedivere, the door to the bedchamber housing my family, the house ... everything. "*How?* And how in hell do I keep them here? Am I supposed to make them my prisoners? Paul—"

I broke off. Paul was going to go ballistic. And then have me committed. And then probably never speak to me again. Ever.

I'd been stunned by Kate's announcement that she'd already brought him, Natalie, and Braden with her and left them in her car on the nearest road to the house, under the protection of wards and two other midwitches.

Too stunned to argue as she and Anne had launched into action, ordering Bedivere to carry the two unconscious adults from the car while Kate carried Braden, and then settling all three into the room next to mine. One room, Anne had decreed, because Paul and Natalie would likely want to keep Braden with them, at least for the moment, and keeping them together would be safest *"in case."*

But my shock was wearing off now, and— *"Jesus,"* I muttered.

"Hah! I knew you had it in you," Edie crowed. *"Now finish. Jesus Christ on a—"*

I was beyond holding back. *"Will* you fuck off," I snarled at my invisible best friend.

Kate, Anne, Keven, and Bedivere all stared at me.

"I didn't mean—" I broke off and glared at the lot of them. "Actually, never mind, because yes, you can all fuck off, too."

"Too?" asked Anne.

I ignored the question. "You haven't answered me. How do I explain—"

"Mom?" Paul's voice broke through mine. "What —where—"

I cringed. Closed my eyes and willed myself to be anywhere but here. Opened them again and found all my companions— including a snarling Bedivere in wolf form, atop his abandoned clothing—staring at a point behind me.

"Fuck," said Edie. *"Fuckity fuck fuck fuck."*

All gazes swiveled to me.

Or maybe that had been me.

"Definitely you," Edie agreed, her tone one of awe. *"Well done, my friend."*

I took a deep breath, curled my hands into fists at my sides, and turned to my son, who stood in the open bedroom door-way, staring white faced at Anne, Kate the cop-slash-midwitch, Keven the living gargoyle, and Bedivere, who had just morphed before his eyes.

"Paul," I said, my voice made tinny by fake cheer. "You're awake."

He slumped to the floor.

"Or not," said Edie.

Keven strode forward wordlessly, picked up my son, and carried him back into the room. She dumped him on the bed again with Natalie and Braden.

CHAPTER 14

I SPENT THE REST OF THE DAY IN MY FAMILY'S BEDCHAMBER, watching over them from a chair beside the window as I waited for them to regain consciousness. I wrestled with my guilt over not being downstairs, helping to plan whatever it was we might do next—*if* there was anything we could do besides sit and wait ... for Lucan, for the Mages, for the other Crones.

But even if I had been with Anne, my brain would have still been here, with Paul and Natalie, fabricating and discarding story after story that I might tell them to explain why they were here, why I was here ... where here was.

I arrived—reluctantly, and only because I could think of no other options—at the conclusion that Anne and Kate were right. I would have to tell them the truth. But holy hell, where would I begin?

Once upon a time, there lived a King named Arthur ...

Edie snorted in my head.

"You have a better idea?" I muttered, resting an elbow on the arm of the wingback chair and rubbing my hand over my eyes.

"How about, 'I'm not the mother you're looking for'?"

I groaned at her corny—and clumsy—*Star Wars* reference. "You, my friend, watched that movie way too many times."

"And you didn't watch it nearly enough. It was a great—"

"Maman?" Natalie's groggy voice came from the bed. "Who are you talking to? And what are you doing in our bedroom?"

My heart dropped to my toes, recovered, and climbed back up to where it belonged. This was it. Showtime. I gathered myself and stood up from the chair, easing upright as my hips protested sitting for too long. It had been hours, I realized, noting the gloom that had descended over the room.

I hobbled to the bedside table and touched the lamp,

keeping my hand on it to adjust the glow to a comfortable level. Propped against the pillows, Natalie blinked at her sleeping husband and child, then at me. Confusion shadowed her normally bright eyes.

"Maman?" she asked again. "This isn't—where are we?"

"My house," I said, even though it wasn't quite the truth anymore. The story I told her would be complicated enough without explaining that part, too. "I—we—brought you here because yours wasn't ..."

"Ours wasn't what?" Alarm flared in her face, and she sat up straighter. "Did something happen to our house again? Another microburst?"

The freak windstorm was the explanation Kate had planted in their memories for what had happened the night the goliath had smashed through their home and stolen Braden from his bed. I shook my head. "No, your house is fine. It's just not— it's not safe for you to be there right now, Natalie. It's safer here."

We hoped.

My daughter-in-law's arm went around her son, tucking him closer to her side. "I don't understand—how is it not safe? What's wrong with it?"

"It's not the house," I reiterated. "It's me—and you—and—"

The sound of a throat being cleared came from the doorway, and I looked over to find Anne with a tray balanced carefully in her one good hand. "This might help," she said. "It will remove the block from some of their memories."

"Some?" I went to take the tray from her as it wobbled in her grip.

"Memories?" Natalie asked from the bed.

"It will let them remember the events without the emotional impact," Anne murmured to me. "We think."

"You think."

"The gargoyle and I worked on it together. She's quite knowledgeable."

The answer wasn't as certain as I would have liked. Or as promising. Tray in hand, I hesitated.

"Maman, what is going on? Who is that? And what memories is she talking about?" Natalie's voice verged on shrill, and Paul stirred in the bed beside her.

I looked down at the two mugs of murky gray liquid on the tray. "Only two?" I asked Anne.

"The little one doesn't need to remember," she said. "He'll adapt without."

"Maman!"

"Nat?" Paul shot up in bed beside her. "What's wro—wait—where the hell are we? *Mom?*"

Faced with little other choice, I took a deep breath, pasted a reassuring smile on my face, and carried the tray to the bedside table. Here went nothing.

It took significant coaxing to get Natalie and Paul to drink the tea Keven and Anne had prepared, but when I flatly refused to explain anything until every last drop was gone, they complied—Natalie with far more grace than my glowering son, who drained his mug and slammed it down on the tray hard enough to crack it.

"There," he snapped. "Satisfied? *Now* will you tell us what the f—heck is going on?"

"Like mother, like son," Edie muttered.

"Hush," I told her absently.

Paul gaped at me. "Don't you dare hush me. I deserve an explanation, damn—" He winced and put a hand to one temple. "Ah!"

Natalie reached out a hand to him. "Paul? What's—" Her other hand shot to her own head. *"Câlice!"* she swore in French. "Maman, what was in that tea?"

I winced in guilty sympathy as each of them cradled their heads in their hands, faces scrunched up in pain. Between them in the bed, Braden slept on. I supposed it was for the best, but how much sedative had Kate given him?

"It's—just give it a minute, and then I'll explain," I said, because there was no point in telling them about magick potions before this one did its work.

Natalie swore again. Even through his discomfort, my son managed to send her a disapproving, sidelong look. "Really, Nat?" he muttered, and then another spasm claimed him, and he groaned.

"Really, Paul?" Edie grumbled. *"I swear he's as bad about that with her as Jeff was with you."*

Except Natalie was way better at handling it than I had been, I thought as my daughter-in-law ignored her husband and let out a string of language that would have sent my uptight old neighbor, Jeanne, stomping from the room in a huff. *Bravo, Natalie*, I thought.

We watched over them together—me at the bedside, Anne just inside the door, Bedivere lurking in the corridor—until their discomfort slowly receded. Natalie was the first to take her hands away from her head. Eyes wide, she stared around the room, taking in the furnishings, the fireplace, the stone walls, me. "Maman—"

"Jesus Christ!" a gaping Paul interrupted. "I remember —*do* I remember? Something took Braden—and there was a wolf—and a stone ... was that a *gargoyle*? And you ..." He trailed off, grappling with the flashes of memory I knew he was experiencing—with what he was seeing and disbelieving in his mind's eye. My heart squeezed in on itself, hating what he had to endure. What he would realize.

What he would think of me.

I didn't have to wait long. His gaze locked on me, and a dozen expressions flickered over his features. Fear. Accusation. Condemnation. "Jesus, Mom—what in hell did you *do* to those people?"

My shoulders hunched under the weight of his judgment. With or without his memories restored, this was not going to be easy for my son. Or for me. Anne came the rest of the way into the room to stand at my side.

"She saved you," she told Paul, "with her magick."

I gave an inward sigh. I wished I'd thought to tell her beforehand that bluntness wouldn't work with Paul. It never had. But it was too late now.

My son's mouth flapped soundlessly for a second. Then he shook his head. "No. No way. Magic doesn't exist. It's—it was a dream. It had to be. Yes. I dreamed it."

Just as you dreamed the ball of fire I conjured in my palm at the coffee shop? I wanted to ask, but Anne forestalled me.

"If that's the case, your wife dreamed the same thing." She nodded at the silent Natalie, who continued to stare at me.

Paul kept shaking his head.

Anne sighed and snapped her fingers, and Bedivere strolled into the room, grinned for the first time since I'd met him, and morphed into his wolf form. My son—my beloved, impossible son who grew more like his father with every passing year— shrieked and scrambled out of the bed to stand on the far side of the bedchamber, well away from his wife and son and the creature his brain deemed to be a threat.

Oh, Paul.

Natalie, on the other hand, didn't seem in the least perturbed. "You're a witch, aren't you?" she asked, her voice filled with wonder. "A real, honest-to-goddess witch."

"It's—" I began, but the word *complicated* died before it was born, and I stared at her, my mouth hanging open. I snapped it closed. "You said honest-to-goddess, not God."

"My grandmother was a witch." She scrambled out of the bed and threw her arms around me. "I *knew* there was a reason I liked you so much when I met you. Will you teach me? Grandmama died when I was young, and I never had the chance to ask her, and—oh!—I'm so excited!"

"Natalie?" Paul croaked, his back pressed against the stone wall beside the window.

"Huzzah!" Edie cackled in my brain.

"It's—I'm not—" I tried without success to disengage myself from Natalie's embrace as she rocked me back and forth in her enthusiasm.

"Wait," she said, pulling back and turning to Anne so suddenly that I almost fell over. "Does this mean you're a witch, too? Did you do—" She pointed at Bedivere's wolf.

He, of course, chose that exact moment to morph back into his human form. His stark naked, very hairy human form.

"Oh," said Natalie. "Oh, my."

"Jee-*sus*," said my son.

"Mommy, why is that man naked?" asked Braden's sleepy voice from the bed.

CHAPTER 15

I STOOPED TO RETRIEVE BEDIVERE'S CLOTHES AND THRUST them at him. "Really?" I muttered.

Bedivere's gray eyes glittered with hard amusement, but they didn't for an instant lose their dangerous glint. He might be having a little fun with this moment, but he still wasn't my friend. I would be wise to remember he wasn't my family's, either. If push came to shove, his bond to Anne—and the memory of the Crone he had once lost—would take precedence over anything and everything else. He took the clothes from me and retreated to the fireplace to dress, watching—always watching—over his shoulder.

I turned back to the others. Natalie had lifted Braden from the bed, his arms wrapped around her neck and his legs all the way around her waist. Sadness tugged at me. When had he gotten so tall that he could do that? I'd missed so much already in just six weeks.

"Look who's here, Bray." She pointed to me, and Braden lifted his head from her shoulder.

"Hi, Grandma," he said. "Is that your boyfriend? Is that why he's naked?"

I choked, Bedivere snorted, and Paul turned bright red. Anne *ahemmed* and steered the conversation back on track.

"We are witches, yes," she answered Natalie's last question, seemingly oblivious to Paul's continued color metamorphosis. He was a rather alarming shade of purple now, and I half-expected him to pass out again, this time from a lack of oxygen.

"But it's rather more complicated than that," Anne continued, "and a great deal more than we can tell you. What you need to know is that we've brought you here because the people who attacked you before are back, and it's not safe for you to stay in town."

Natalie's lips formed a silent "o". Braden's eyes went wide.

"You're a witch, Grandma? Can I ride on your broom?"

Before I could answer—or think of an answer—Paul stalked over to join us, blustering every step of the way.

"You—we—no," he said. He stood over his wife, arms akimbo and waving wildly. "Nat, you can't actually believe what she's saying. Are you kidding me? We're not staying here. We're not staying anywhere but our own home. What about my life? My job?"

"We've already taken care of it," I assured him, trying not to grimace. *His* life? *His* job?

"He's his father's son, all right," said Edie.

"We? We who?" he demanded. He set his hands on his hips and turned his attention on me, his stance aggressive. "Tell me, Mom. How in hell have you taken care of *my* life?"

Because Braden was staring at me and his angry father, I swallowed the retort I wanted to make and kept my tone level, conciliatory. "We told your office you were called away to a family emergency. Kate Abraham—the police officer who took you back to your house that night, remember?—took care of the arrangements, and she brought some clothes—"

"She—a *cop* is one of you?" Paul raked all his fingers through his hair. Then he waved me off in disgust. "No. No way. This is bullshit. I don't know what was in that tea you gave us, but you're all insane, and I'm done. I'm going home, and I'm taking—"

A half-dressed Bedivere stepped between him and Natalie as he reached to take Braden from her. Paul shuffled backward, away from the carpet-covered chest, then recovered and drew himself up to his full six-foot-plus height. He still came up several inches shorter than Bedivere, so he threw back his shoulders for good measure, and curled his hands into fists at his sides.

"Get out of my way," he snapped, "or I swear I will take you out."

Braden whimpered and turned his face into his mother's neck.

"Paul!" she hissed.

Her husband ignored her, half-raising his fists and shifting his feet into a fighting stance. Calmy, Bedivere pulled his loose-fitting shirt on over his head with his one hand and slid his arms into the gathered sleeves. He tugged the garment into place around his hips. Then he looked down at my puffed-up son and smiled.

"If Lady Anne says you're staying," he said, "then you're staying."

My son vibrated with fury—or maybe indecision—and whirled to face me.

"Damn it to hell, Mom, you can't possibly think you can keep us prisoner here!"

"If you'd just listen," I began, but my son pushed past Bedivere—who, of course, made no effort to stop him this time—and came to stand toe-to-toe with me.

"I'm done listening," he ground out. "I've been cutting you all kinds of slack since your house burned down and Edie died, but enough is enough. You and your freaky friends are taking us home—*now*—and I'm calling Dad, and we're getting you the help you—"

"That's enough, Paul," said Natalie. Braden still in her arms, she wedged herself between us.

"This is none of your business, Nat."

"Of course it's my business. I'm half of this marriage, and Braden is my son as well as yours, and you're scaring him half to death right now. Back. Off."

As petite as she was, my daughter-in-law bristled with an anger many times that of her husband, and I watched in surprise —no, shock—as Paul visibly deflated in the face of it. Natalie turned her back on her husband and faced me and Anne. Her gaze fastened on me. "Tell me, Maman," she said. "Are we really in danger?"

"Yes," I said. "I think so. But I can't explain—"

"You don't need to. You asked me once before if I trust you, and I do. I remember everything, and—" She broke off with a shudder, her lively face turning somber, then finished simply, "We'll stay as long as you think we need to."

"Like hell we will," Paul growled. "Those aren't memories, Nat, they're hallucinations. They put something in that damned tea!"

"The tea removed the block that was put in place before," Anne told him, her tone taking on a sharp edge, "but that was all. It didn't give you any memories you didn't already have."

"Before? You did something to us before? Braden, too? What the hell kind of people are you?"

"The kind who are trying to save your asses," Edie grumbled, *"pontificating little—"*

"He's still my son," I reminded her in my head, and she snorted.

"And I still should've given him more detentions when I had the chance."

I didn't argue.

Paul was still ranting, throwing around words like *cult* and *investigation, sue,* and *see you in court.* I took a deep breath and tried to cut across the outpouring, to reason with him. But he just got louder and nastier, and my own unpleasant memories began to surface. I knew all too well where he'd learned this kind of bullying behavior, and—

"Enough!" His wife rounded on him, fury in every taut line of her body. "She's your *mother*, Paul. How dare you speak to her that way? And in front of Braden! How would you like it if he talked to me like that one day?"

Paul seemed taken aback by the question, and as he looked at the son hiding his face from him, I knew the idea hadn't even occurred to him. Then he rallied. "It's not the—"

"It's exactly the same," Natalie countered. "And you know as well as I do that none of what you're saying is even true. Your mother would *never* do anything to hurt you. You remember what happened that night. I know you remember, because I can see it in your eyes. What your mother did that night was to save us—you, me, Braden. That thing that took him was real. It would have killed him if she hadn't stopped it, and if there's even the remotest chance it might come after him again, there's no way I'm going back to the house. If Maman says we're safer here, then we're safer here."

"But I—"

"I'm staying." Natalie held her son tight and lifted her chin high, daring him to argue. "And so is Braden." They stared at one another for a tense minute, Paul's jaw flexing and releasing. At last, looking around at their audience, he backed down, but only a little.

"This isn't over," he muttered.

Natalie's little head-toss said otherwise, and it was all I could do not to burst into applause. How different life might have been, I thought—and how different my son might have been, too—if I'd been able to stand up to Paul's father like that more often.

"Or at all," Edie volunteered.

Or at all.

"Well," said Anne. "Now we've settled the matter, we'll leave you to get comfortable. You're free to roam the house, of course, and if you need anything, you can pull the cord by the bed. The gargoyle will look after you."

"Her name is Keven," I told Natalie. "The gargoyle, I mean."

"I remember," Natalie said, hugging her son close. "She was kind to us that night, especially Braden. How could we forget all of that?" She gave her head a little shake and smiled at me with the utmost faith shining in her eyes. "Never mind. I said I trust you, Maman, and I do."

I knew she meant well, but a shiver crept over me, and my

stomach did an uneasy flip. I could summon neither an answering smile nor words of my own in response because, dear goddess, what if I couldn't live up to that trust? What if—

"Claire?" Anne's voice interrupted my silent panic, and I realized that she and Bedivere were already in the hall waiting for me.

"I'll send up some dinner," I said, "and maybe you'd like to join us for breakfast tomorrow."

Natalie's smile widened, and she nodded vigorously. Seeing her try to compensate for her husband's behavior hurt my heart. How had I never noticed the fallout of my own failed marriage in theirs?

I gave my grandson and Natalie a quick group hug, bypassed my stiff, self-righteous son because I didn't quite trust myself not to smack him upside the head instead of hugging him, and made good my escape.

CHAPTER 16

"GRANDMA, DID KNOW THERE'S A TALKING STATUE THAT lives here?" Braden burst into the dining room the next morning in a whirlwind of excitement, running around the table past Anne to launch himself at me. "And Merlin is here, too! Is this your new house?"

"Merlin?" Anne's hand froze with the teacup halfway to her lips as her amusement gave way to shock and horror. Beside her, before I could so much as open my mouth to explain, Bedivere morphed into his wolf and bolted from the room.

Shit. He was not going to be happy about this.

Natalie skidded into the room a split-second later. "Braden, I told you, no running in the house," she panted. She shot me an apologetic look. "I'm sorry, Maman. He got away on me."

She made no mention of having crossed paths with Bedivere's wolf. He really did move as fast as Lucan. Perhaps even faster.

"It's fine," I told my daughter-in-law, lifting my grandson onto my lap. I grimaced at Anne. "He meant the cat. I named him back when I thought Merlin was the good guy."

"And a wolf, too!" Braden exclaimed, tapping my shoulder for my attention. "I saw it in the hall outside our bedroom last night. Can I get my own room today? Daddy snores."

"You changed it, I hope." Anne's cup clattered against the saucer as she set it down. "The cat's name?"

Guilt twinged through me at having inadvertently caused the minor panic. "Of course," I hastened to assure her. "He's Mergan, now." I looked down at Braden. "Can you remember that, sweetie? Can you call the kitty Mergan from now on?"

"Mergan?" Anne echoed, one brow raised.

"That's a funny name," Braden said.

"It was a funny time," I replied, tickling him in the ribs and making him squeal. Not quite managing to block out the memories of my run through the gauntlet of gnomes that had preceded the name change. Or using the poor cat in his carrier as a sledgehammer of sorts.

It was no wonder Mergan had abandoned me and made Keven his new person when we'd arrived at the house. I'd long since given up hope that he would forgive me. He and the gargoyle were practically inseparable, though Keven would never have admitted to it.

I brought my attention back to my wriggling grandson. "Can you remember to call him that for me? Mergan?"

Braden nodded, and then as the dining room door opened and Keven came in with platters in hand and the ever-present ginger cat wrapped around her shoulders, he shouted, "Merlin!" and slid off my lap to run and greet the feline.

I wheezed. Anne winced. Natalie looked confused by the to-do being made. Keven rolled her stone eyes.

"You think I didn't know?" she asked, looking at me for the first time in almost two weeks. "Seriously, what kind of name is *Mergan*, anyway?" She heaved a sigh and turned her head to the cat riding on her. "Gus. That's your name now, understand?"

Merlin-Mergan-Gus yawned his diffidence, and the gargoyle transferred her gaze to the five-year-old bundle of energy bouncing at her side and patting her arm to get her attention.

"What?" she grumbled.

"I want a new name, too," Braden declared.

"Fine." Keven slammed a platter of sausages and eggs onto the table. The toast platter followed it. "You can be Pest. Now, for goddess's sake, sit down and stop moving."

She lumbered back toward the door, pausing to look back at Natalie. "We'll start after breakfast."

"Start what?" I asked as the door swung shut behind her.

"Herbs," Natalie replied gleefully, scooping up her son and plonking him into an empty chair. "Keven said she'd teach me."

She took the chair beside Braden and reached for the eggs. Behind her, the dining room door slammed open again, making all of us jump.

A naked Bedivere stalked in and growled at me, "The gargoyle said you named the cat *Merlin*?"

"It was all a misunderstanding, Bedivere," Anne told him.

"There is no misunderstanding that name, milady," he replied to her but continued glaring at me. "Or the person who bestows it."

I opened my mouth to object, but Anne forestalled me. "I said it was a misunderstanding," she repeated, "and that's what it was. That's *all* it was, please."

The *please* gave a thin veil of politeness to her words, but the underlying command was still clear. Bedivere flashed me a last look of dislike wrapped in suspicion, then gave Anne a stiff nod.

"As you wish, milady."

Natalie leaned toward me as he snatched up his clothes and began dressing again. "Is he always like that?" she murmured.

"Angry? Pretty much," I whispered back.

"I meant naked."

I sighed. "Pretty much," I said again. "You get used to it."

She seemed doubtful, but a request from Braden for toast forestalled further discussion, and she turned away to tend to him. Bedivere tugged his shirt over his head and resumed his seat to Anne's left. Anne pushed the platter of eggs closer to him, and breakfast commenced.

The sixth and last place setting at the table, however, sat unclaimed.

"Is your husband joining us?" Anne asked, pushing the teapot toward me but looking at Natalie.

"He might be down later," Natalie said, scooping scrambled eggs onto Braden's plate. She carefully didn't look in my direction as she added, "Or I might take a plate up to him. He ... has a bit of a headache this morning."

"Of course," said Anne. "There was a lot of excitement last

night. Let the gargoyle know if he needs something for the headache. She's very good at remedies."

PAUL'S "HEADACHE" DIDN'T IMPROVE. FOR THE FIRST couple of days, Natalie carried meals up to him from the dining room. On the third day, Keven simply set a tray for him in the kitchen and took it up herself when the rest of us sat down to eat —and I stopped asking about him. My son had learned passive-aggressive behavior from a master, and I'd had plenty of practice at being on the receiving end of the silent treatment. As long as Paul was being decent to his wife and son—and Natalie assured me he was, because I made a point of asking—then it was best to wait for him to get over sulking in his own time.

But while my son was a lost cause for the moment, refusing to leave his room or speak to me, my daughter-in-law and grandson were enthralled with their new space. Braden seemed to know instinctively to stay out of Bedivere's way, but he trotted after Keven like a puppy, constantly underfoot and oblivious—as only a five-year-old could be—to the gargoyle's short responses to his endless questions and run-on commentary. By day three, Keven seemed to have adjusted, and I suspected she'd even begun to secretly enjoy my grandson's adoration.

I'd thanked her for her patience with him as she cleared the lunch dishes this afternoon, and for the first time since Lucan's departure, she had actually looked at me rather than past me. Granted, her shrug hadn't encouraged further discussion, but I liked to think—hope—that she might have been at least a little pleased. I heaved an inner sigh, hating that things with her continued to be so—

Goddess, I was tired of the word *complicated*, but it was honestly the only word that fit. The adjective described all my relationships, when I thought about it. The one with my son, the ones with not-my gargoyle and currently absent not-my protector, the one with Anne, and most definitely the one with Bedivere, whose suspicion of me seemed to increase by the day.

And then ... then, there was the relationship with my magick, which continued to be the single most complicated thing in my life. Anne, bless her soul, refused to give up on me. Hour after hour, she worked at teaching me the simplest of spells. Hour after hour, I failed to master any of them.

For her part, Natalie took to herbs and potions like the proverbial duck to water. I tried hard not to be envious of my daughter-in-law's skills, but so far, I was failing.

Rather miserably, if I were honest.

And behind all of it, lurking in the shadows of my magickal practice (or lack thereof), my visits with Natalie and Braden, and my failed attempts to coax my son from his room, lay the emptiness in the house that was Lucan's absence. We didn't talk about it, Anne and I, but I knew she marked the number of days he'd been gone the same way I did.

Well, maybe not in quite the same aching loss way.

But close enough.

Because each day he remained absent was another that the other Crones remained missing; another when she was ostensibly the only one of the four still alive; another when the cloud of my shortcomings grew ever darker.

That last thought had been on my mind ever since Lucan had left, intermingled with worries about the safety of my family since their arrival. It sat uppermost now, as I paused in my gathering of herbs on the afternoon of their third day in the house.

Standing in the garden that continued to grow as if oblivious to the shorter days and encroaching cold, I eased my spine upright. What *would* happen if he returned empty-handed, unable to locate the other Crones? Or if he did find them, and—

I shuddered and let my gaze travel over the trees just beyond the garden's rock wall. The brilliant autumn colors were so at odds with the shadows overhanging my life and with the surly gazes that followed my every movement—the feral Bedivere's no matter where I turned, and Paul's from his window whenever I was in the garden.

And then there was the distance that remained between me and Keven despite her acceptance of my family—well, of Natalie and Braden, at any rate. And the fact that I hadn't seen a single crow since the Morrigan's gown had dissolved into the murder in my room that night. No crows, no movement from the Mages that Kate and her fellow midwitches were monitoring in town, no sign of impending attack. It was as if my entire world had been put on hold. Thrust into limbo.

It was unsettling.

"What if it's a trap?" My own words had haunted me relentlessly since my argument with Kate, even though the intervening days had proved her right. Just as there had been no Mage activity in town, neither had there been any sign of them near the house, as she'd predicted.

I stooped to pick up the basket of herbs and the staff I'd laid on the ground by my feet. I still couldn't wrap my head around the idea that it was my presence that deterred them, but—

A new possibility surfaced, and I paused, staff and basket in one hand, the knife I'd used for cutting the herbs in the other. What if my presence had nothing to do with it—or, at least, not in the way we'd thought? What if it *had* been a trap, but one designed not to attack me, but to keep me here? To ensure I remained with my family, rather than—

I rolled my eyes and sighed. *Really, Claire? First you're not good enough to be the reason the Mages stay away, and now you're so good they want to keep you here?* Talk about delusions of grandeur. I tucked the knife in beside the verbena and yarrow, transferred my staff to that hand, and started back toward the kitchen.

Looking up, I saw Paul at his window and raised my staff hand in greeting. The curtain dropped back into place, and I sighed again. His father's record for not speaking to me after a disagreement had been seven days. At this rate, Paul was on track to meet or beat that.

Awesome.

I shivered in the breeze. I hadn't worn my cloak, and now that I'd stopped bending and stretching, I was cooling off rapidly. I picked my way through the carrot patch toward the center path leading to the kitchen door. Bedivere had muttered a suggestion at breakfast this morning that we should stop catering to Paul and let him come out when he got hungry enough. I'd glossed over the comment at the time because Braden was at the table with us, but the shifter had a point. It might be time to treat my son like the spoiled brat he'd become.

Or the one he'd always been, but I'd never noticed before.

I stepped over the last row of carrots and onto the path.

And then a crow cawed.

THE SINGLE, HOARSE CALL ECHOED THROUGH THE AUTUMN-quiet woods, dying away even as my head snapped around and my steps froze.

I stared in the direction of the sound, my gaze probing the trees and their shadows, but I found no bird hidden among them. No movement other than the faint breeze stirring through the leaves still clinging to branches, sending bits of crimson and gold and russet drifting earthward. There was no second call.

I hunched my shoulders. Had it been my imagination? Paranoia? Both? I made myself loosen the fingers holding the wicker basket handle, but my hours of training, even in Lucan's absence, kept my grip on the staff firm. Ready. Perhaps it had been an actual crow, and not one of mine. Because actual ones still existed, I reminded myself. I knew that because I'd sometimes seen the others look up and track their paths across the sky when they heard their calls.

The ones that appeared only to me numbered in the tens—and they were silent. Except, I reminded myself, for the one that had called out to me when I had first tried to find the house. The one that had shown me the gate and the path beyond.

I surveyed the woods a second time, but no bird showed itself, and no path appeared. Definitely paranoia. I took a deep, settling breath and started again for the house.

And then, from the corner of my eye, I saw it.

A shimmering, gossamer-fine ribbon that started at the house and stretched across the garden and into the trees. It flickered and danced with the palest rainbow of colors: there, not there, there again. I stared at it, holding the breath I'd inhaled. It was ... what? Beautiful, indisputably. Fragile, possibly. Real? I had no idea.

I set the basket on the ground and picked my way back through the carrots toward the ribbon. As I drew nearer, I saw that it didn't shimmer so much as it undulated, writhing like a translucent, slow-moving snake that had neither head nor tail. A snake made of tiny bits of light, each hovering near the others but not touching. Each ... alive?

It crossed my mind that they might be wards, but I dismissed the idea. I'd seen wards—before I'd destroyed them— and they were larger than these, more like fireflies. And even if wards had been willing to come this close to me, they didn't behave like this. They formed net-like structures around things, not—

In the woods, the crow cawed again, and the tiny hairs stirred along my arms.

I reached out with my free hand and watched my fingers slip into the midst of the moving pinpricks of color. It was like dipping them in the half-frozen river in January. I pulled back again with a surprised inhale, my skin tingling and burning with cold. The ribbon pulsed as if it had felt my touch. Responded to it.

A faint scent, woodsy and a little musky, teased my nose and made me frown. I knew that smell—or felt certain that I should. But from where?

Lucan.

The thought of him blindsided me. It took a second to process as my brain cells collided with one another in confusion. Slowly, they sorted themselves out, and I caught my breath as remembrance gelled. That scent—I'd smelled it before, every time Lucan and I practiced with the staffs. A mix of heat and sweat—and the smell of the woods through which he ran as a wolf that never quite seemed to fade from him.

I stepped closer to the ribbon and leaned in to test the air again. My stomach did a little flip, and a sudden pang shot through me. That was definitely Lucan's scent. I was sure of it. It permeated the entire construct, and goddess, but it made me miss him again. Still. More.

But it wasn't just his scent. It was ... I frowned. It was *him*. The ribbon vibrated with his presence, his very essence, as if he were somehow caught within—

"Oh, for ..." I let my growl trail off, straightening again, all kinds of irritated with myself for taking so long to figure it out. It was a ley line. And not just any ley line, but the one Lucan must have followed when he went to look for the others. But why was I only seeing it now, and why only the one?

I looked over one shoulder, then the other, then studied the house, which Keven had told me sat at an intersection of lines. I hadn't the foggiest idea how many lines constituted an intersection, but no matter how hard I looked, I found no others. The hairs lifted again along my arms. One ley line. One crow, heard but not seen. One shifter who had yet to return, with or without news of the others, who might need help.

Lucan's presence grew stronger with every pulse of the ley line's energy, tugging at me with invisible, insistent fingers. *Follow me*, it said.

"Anne," my Claire-voice countered. *"You should tell Anne."*

I might have agreed with it, if the ley line hadn't suddenly dimmed, shifted, and then sputtered out of existence. The air in my lungs froze solid and I stared in shock at where it had been a scant second before and now just ... wasn't. Where Lucan had been and—

Lucan.

The ribbon winked to life again, but it was thin and watery, its colors washed out almost to white, and its movements jerky and uncoordinated—and Lucan's presence within it was gone. I sucked in a shallow breath, dread gripping my heart in a cold, tight fist.

"Anne," my Claire-voice reminded me.

Lucan, I responded. And without so much as a backward glance—because I didn't dare take my eyes off the ley line again —I gripped my staff at the ready in both hands and stepped into the magick.

CHAPTER 17

I DON'T KNOW WHAT I EXPECTED LEY TRAVEL TO BE LIKE, but if I'd taken the time to imagine it, I would never have dreamed—*could* never have dreamed—that it would feel as if I had been ripped limb from limb, shredded into a thousand pieces, and then dissolved in acid.

The agony was so complete that I couldn't even scream. It sucked every molecule of air from my lungs and all coherent thought from my brain. It stole my capacity to feel anything but *it* in my every fiber, my every pore, my very soul. Until I didn't just feel it, I became it.

And then it became more.

If I could have formed the idea, I would have wished for death. If I could have found the words, I would have *begged* for death. But I couldn't, and so I endured. For how long, I had no idea. Seconds, perhaps. An eternity, maybe. When you become your own agony, time doesn't matter. Nothing matters. Nothing until a tiny, distant part of you notices you're still alive—and then you begin to surface, reliving the entire process in reverse.

There was a sudden tug sideways, like the pull of a rope, and then the ribbon spat me out at last onto a cold stone floor in the pitch dark. I landed on my hands and knees with a grunt, staff clutched in frozen fingers so that my knuckles struck first—and hard. My knees didn't fare much better, but for a moment, I stayed where I was, remembering how to breathe and almost reveling in my discomfort. The entirely bearable, not brain-melting discomfort. Bruised knees and skinned knuckles? Pshaw.

A semi-hysterical giggle rose in my chest. I swallowed it, for two reasons: first, I didn't think it wise to announce my presence until I knew where I'd landed and who else might be in the vicinity; and second, I was pretty sure there *was* someone else in the vicinity.

Or something.

A scrape of metal against metal grated through the dark, and the threatening giggle turned to a hard lump lodged at the base of my throat. I froze, all my senses on high alert—or at least the functional ones, because try as I might, sight was useless in the inky blackness. I did, however, hear the rasp of breathing and the rustle of movement. And I could smell something. A lot of something.

I focused on my olfactory system, sifting through what it brought me. Mildew. The stench of urine. A rot I didn't want to identify. And underlying it all, so faint I almost missed it, the woodsy, musky scent that had brought me here. The metallic scrape came again, and I scrambled to my feet, using my staff to support me as I swayed, unable to find my sense of place in the dark.

Lucan. It had to be. But was he alone? Still here? Alive? Or ....

There was only one way to find out.

While I still hadn't managed to produce more than a ball of flame so far—not on purpose, anyway, I thought, sidestepping the memory of the kitchen incident—I could at least do that much reliably. I cupped a hand and held it out, palm up, then reached into my core for the heat that resided there. It wasn't as warm as usual—no wonder, after my disassembly—and it took a moment to coax it to life so that I could begin drawing it out to my surface.

I directed the heat to my outstretched hand, and a tiny flame flickered to life in it. I frowned and focused harder, impatient with it. With myself. Damn it, but I was getting tired of not being able to do the simplest things with the magick I was supposed to have—especially when I needed it the way I did now because *Lucan*. As if feeding on my anxiety, the flame suddenly flared high and hot, and I realized the heat I'd called was rising fast in me. Too fast.

"Emotional," whispered my Claire-voice. *"You're too emotional."*

You think? I swallowed a harsh laugh at the obviousness of her—my?—observation. I focused on slowing my breathing, tamping down the threatening edge of panic, tempering my fear of what I would find.

Lucan.

My breathing evened out. My heart rate followed suit. The flame settled down and became a bright glow akin to a lantern. A tiny pride sparked in me at the control I'd managed, but I put it aside and held up the flame so I could see my surroundings. I would have time later to revel in my success, small though it might be. After I'd found—oh goddess, what *was* this place?

My stomach churned as I turned in a circle. My light played across filthy stone walls dark with damp, a rusted metal bucket overflowing with excrement and urine, a hunk of rotted meat crawling with maggots. I retched at the latter, pressing the back of my staff-holding hand to my mouth. To say I was horrified would have been the understatement of the century. Especially when it was Lucan's presence in the ley line that had brought me here.

And then I saw the bed and the still figure lying on it, and my heart plummeted. With a shaking hand, I held the light out as far as I could and peered into the dark it tried to pierce. In the shadows, I made out the links of a chain, a manacle, a skeletally thin wrist covered in skin too pale to be Lucan's, and a body curled on its side, facing away from me and covered in fabric too flimsy to be of any protection against the damp chill permeating the cell.

I let myself dwell for a moment on the *not Lucan* part of my observations, then inched closer. Not Lucan, perhaps, but definitely someone who needed help. My foot landed on something spongy, and I looked down to find myself standing on a dead rat.

"Cheesy rice on a cracker!" I hissed, dancing backward.

"Who's there?" a woman's voice croaked, sounding rusty from disuse. The figure on the ramshackle metal bed pushed itself up on one elbow, eyes shielded from the brightness of my flame by a wrinkled hand that was claw-like from emaciation. "Declare yourself!"

I opened my mouth to reply, but my words were buried beneath layers of revulsion as I took in her appearance. Long, gray braids hung limp and dull over the shoulders of a thin, filthy nightgown—or at least, what remained of a nightgown; her legs stuck out from the bottom like twigs; the skin of her face sagged across hollowed cheeks; and open sores on her lips oozed pus.

The cell had made me want to throw up. Its occupant made me want to cry.

The woman lowered the hand shielding her eyes, and the shadow it cast across her torso moved with it. Something on her chest glinted in the light of my flame. The world shifted beneath my feet.

A pendant.

Dear goddess, she wore a Crone's pendant.

My hand went to my own, hidden beneath my blouse. "You're one of us," I whispered.

For a moment, we stared at one another in shock, and I honestly wasn't sure which one of us was more surprised by the other's presence. She was the first to react, pushing back on the bed as far as the manacle would let her go and clenching the pendant in her fist.

"Go to hell," she hissed. "I don't care how many times you ask, Mage, I'm damned if I will hand it over to him!"

Mage? Here? I gave an involuntary jump and held my flame higher as I cast about in the shadows for another person. But we were alone. I shined the light back on her—on the sunken eyes, the obvious signs of dehydration and starvation. It was no wonder she was hallucinating.

I shook my head and injected all the reassurance I could summon into my voice. "I'm not—I'm—my name is Claire. Claire Emerson. I'm one of you. I'm a Crone." I dug beneath my shirt and pulled out my pendant, holding it up so that the flame sparkled off its surface. "See?"

It didn't have the effect I expected. Her face crumpled with despair; hopelessness welled in the tears in her eyes. Then she pressed her lips together, bitterness in their line.

"Treachery," she whispered. "Deceit. You may have gotten one pendant, Mage, but I'll still not give you mine."

"I'm not—" I broke off, then changed tactics. "I don't want your pendant, I promise. I didn't even know you were here. I came looking for a friend of mine, a protector. I followed him through the ley lines."

She hesitated, and faint interest sparked in her eyes. "A protector?"

"Lucan, protector of the Earth Crone."

The hopelessness returned, and she turned her face away. "I have no protector."

Oh dear goddess ... *this* was the Earth Crone? No wonder Lucan's trail had led me—Lucan. My heart shredded and my knees sagged. I leaned on my staff, swaying. I'd followed his scent here—his presence. That meant he had to have been here. But if he had, he would never have left his Crone. Not voluntarily. That could mean only one—

"—if I had, I wouldn't be here."

I locked my knees and stopped swaying. "What?"

The woman sighed, a whispery rasp of sound. "I said, perhaps if I'd had my protector, I wouldn't be here."

"He hasn't been here?" The flame in my hand trembled with the effort of holding it aloft for so long, and I lowered it to waist height and rolled my shoulder to ease the cramp threatening there. "But I followed him here through the ley line—I could smell him in it. Feel his presence."

"That's not possible. Crones cannot travel the lines on their own." Suspicion reared its head in her expression again; puzzlement followed. "But neither can Mages."

"But Keven said we can tap into the ley."

"Keven?"

"My—your—" I stopped as the Crone in the bed was wracked by a rattling cough. Goddess, where were my priorities? I should be thinking about how to get her out of here and back to the house. She needed healing—and food—not questions and explanations. But how? She would never survive going back through the ley with me—not in her condition. I was pretty sure I'd barely survived it myself.

Her coughing spell ended, and she lay down again, head cradled on her arm because there was no pillow, eyes closed, breathing labored.

I was going to need help.

I stepped over the dead rat and crossed the dank cell to her bedside, carefully breathing through my mouth and not my nose as I lowered myself to sit beside her in the filth she occupied. I leaned my staff against the bed and rested my flame-bearing hand in my lap. Maintaining its glow was harder than it should have been, and I took a moment to steady it again before I looked over at the woman it illuminated.

"What's your name?" I asked softly.

"Elysabeth," she murmured, eyes still closed. "I am Elysabeth, Crone of Earth. And you, Claire Emerson, you are the Fire Crone, I presume?"

"Not exactly. It's ..." The words *it's complicated* hovered on the tip of my tongue, but I made myself say other words instead. "I'm actually the Fifth Crone."

Her eyes snapped open, and I saw they were a soft, gentle brown—clouded now with pain and exhaustion, but capable, I suspected, of great sparkle at another time. A better time.

"Seriously?"

"Yes, but I'm not very good at it, I'm afraid, so I'm not going to be able to get you out of here on my own. I'm going to have to find the others first." I could see the questions at war behind her expression and was relieved when she opted for one of the easier ones to answer—my Cronehood not being it.

"They're missing? All of them?"

"Air and Fire are. Anne—the Water Crone—is at my—your —house. She was badly injured in the—an—attack." Wow. I was positively eloquent, wasn't I? I took a breath and tried again. "The three of them were at Anne's house, waiting for you, when the Mages attacked with their goliath. The Crones scattered. Bedivere, Lady Anne's protector, managed to get her to your house, and Keven—your gargoyle—is healing her." She was also caring for my family, but I didn't think Elysabeth needed to know that I'd turned her home into a safe house. Besides, it was time for a question of my own. "How long have you been here?"

"Too long," she said. "Weeks, I think. I have no way of knowing."

"You look ..."

"Like I'm dying of starvation?" She gave a short, bitter laugh, and her breath wafted over me, sickly sweet with the odor of impending death. "That's his plan."

"I don't under—" My words dropped off as I remembered sitting at the kitchen table with Keven and Lucan while they told me about Morok's quest to open a portal to the Camlann splinter, where half his power had been trapped in the original split caused by Morgana and the Morrigan. Keven had told me that Morok needed the power of the Crone pendants to accomplish his task, and that there were two ways he could get them: *either before a pendant chooses its new Crone, or if a Crone chooses to give it to him.*

"I refused to hand it over," Elysabeth said quietly, as if she'd read my mind, "and they got tired of trying to convince me."

"Dear goddess," I breathed, looking around the befouled cell again. At the excrement in the corner, as far from the bed as the manacle would allow. At the overflowing bucket of—I gagged. "Is *that* how you survived?"

"My own urine? Goddess, no. I'd have been dead already if I did that. There's a spot on the wall behind me where moisture seeps through. It's been just enough to keep me alive. That, and sheer fucking stubbornness, I suspect." She gave another short laugh that ended again in a coughing fit.

She lay back on the bed until it passed, then turned sober eyes on me. Sad eyes. Nearly defeated eyes. "But between you and me, Claire Emerson, I don't think I can hold out much longer."

"Why didn't they just ..."

Her lips twisted, and a crusted-over sore split wide. She inhaled sharply and put the back of her free hand against it. "Why don't they kill me? Goddess, are you really that naive? You do know who the Mages are, don't you?"

"Servants of Morok?" I meant it to be a statement, but there was a definite question mark at the end because I realized that no, I really didn't.

"Servants," she said, "of a god who's had it in for women ever since Morgana beat his ass."

CHAPTER 18

I BLINKED AT ELYSABETH, NOT SURE QUITE WHAT TO MAKE of the bitter words that sounded too simple to be a real explanation. She stared back at me, her gaze unflinching.

"I—they—you—" It took me a moment to stop flapping my mouth and pull actual words from it. "You're serious."

She chuckled, a dry whisper of sound that ended on an equally dry cough. "You're surprised?"

"I ... don't know. Maybe a little?"

Elysabeth motioned for help, and I slid a gentle arm behind her, easing her into a half-sitting position against the wall behind her, praying I didn't break anything while doing so. She felt so damned fragile.

"This entire war boils down to a struggle for control," she muttered when she was upright. "Morok lost to Morgana, and he's been losing to the Crones ever since, and all of this—us, them—it all comes down to power. The Mages haven't killed me because they take pleasure in my suffering, and in their ability to cause it. Their god is sick and bitter and twisted, and he has told them lies for centuries—millennia—that have made them sick and bitter and twisted, too."

My skin crawled, turning cold, then hot, then cold again. The flame in my palm dimmed. Flickered. I focused on steadying it. On breathing. Almost every day before I'd gone to the house in the woods, I had read the headlines in my newspaper. The articles that followed them. The stories buried on the back pages. I knew humanity was capable of every kind of atrocity, imaginable or otherwise. But I'd never come face to face with its monstrousness. Never sat beside it on a bed. Never gagged on its smell.

"I've shocked you," she said.

"Yes. No. Maybe a little." I turned my gaze back to the skin-covered skeleton in the bed. "You're not just talking about Mages, are you?"

Elysabeth's brown eyes met mine, and I saw stories buried in them, just as I had in the back pages of the paper. "No," she said. "I'm not."

"But there are good men out there, too."

"Not all men?" she asked wryly. Another coughing fit wracked her frame, and it took longer this time for her to catch her breath. I would need to leave soon. She summoned a tired smile. "Yes, there are good men out there. Strong men. Just as there are weak women—some of them even Mages themselves. But the thing about lies is how insidious they are. How real they feel. They can get inside even the strongest mind and cause doubt. Uncertainty. Silence. And that's all it takes to feed the machine. Weak men take control, fear robs women of their strength and they turn away from the craft; the Mages grow stronger; the pendants choose new Crones; we take away another bit of Morok's power, another slice of the world; and the cycle continues."

Until now. Until me.

Theoretically.

I turned away from the thought, nowhere near ready to tread that path. Not yet. Not now. I pointed to her manacled wrist. "Are you sure you can't—?"

She lifted it a few inches from the bed, and I saw the raw, oozing flesh that marked her efforts to free herself. The chain rattled as she dropped her hand back to the bed. "I'm sure."

"How did they get it on you?"

"Damned if I know. I've been wracking my brain, but I have no idea how they even found me," she said. "Mages have never been able to track us like that; they've always had to wait until we gather and begin raising our powers for the split, and by then, it's been too late. It happened so fast, I didn't have a chance to fight back—or run. I barely had a chance to come to terms with the pendant choosing me, let alone go in search of my house or my protector. Someone knocked at the door, I opened it, and *wham*. When I woke up, I was wearing this, and my connection to magick was ... muted, I suppose you'd say. I can still feel it—and Earth—but I can't touch either of them. This"—she rattled her chain again—"has to be Morok's own handiwork."

Morok, who would hide in the shadows and let his Mages do his dirty work until he had what he wanted. And right now, he already had one Crone.

"And you?" Elysabeth eyed me. "You're sure you're really the Fifth?"

"I'm not sure of anything," I said, wondering what it might have been like to know what the pendant was when it arrived—to know what I was supposed to do with it. "But yes, that's what I've been told."

"What did you mean when you said you're not very good at it?"

I got to use my stock phrase at last. "It's complicated," I said. "I'm working on it."

"But you traveled the ley lines on your own. Without a protector."

Traveled didn't seem to fully encompass the experience I'd had, but I nodded anyway.

"Huh," she said. "Then I suspect you're better than you think you are." She reached out her free hand and rested it on my arm. "Claire, Morok won't stop until he has all four pendants. You need to find the others and make sure they're safe. Make sure they're not"—she held up her manacled wrist—"like me."

I stared at the flame I still held in my lap. "Elysabeth, can the others—can just three ..."

"Can three Crones split the world on their own?" She finished the question I couldn't bring myself to ask. "No. The power needed is enormous. It requires all four elements. Morok can't do anything with my pendant alone, but if he gets it, the

Crones are finished. They'll lose what little edge the world has against him. Every one of them, now and in the future—assuming the pendants even choose future ones—will spend her life on the defensive and nothing more."

And goddess knew my own power wasn't stable enough to be able to raise the Earth element in Elysabeth's stead. I squared my shoulders and took a deep breath, my outward calm belying the quivering, jelly-like mass at my core as I quailed from the responsibility I faced. Was it just me, or did that purpose I'd wished for on my sixtieth birthday become more overwhelming by the day?

"One thing at a time," an inner voice said. Not my Claire- or Edie-voice, but the other one. My ancestors' collective voice, Edie had said. Thousands of witches who had gone before me. It was good to hear from them again, especially now that I knew they were real, relatively speaking, and not just another sign of me losing my grip. They were also right.

First things first. I had to find the others. No, wait. First, I had to survive the trip back through the ley.

"Well, then." I shored up my resolve with false cheer. "I guess I'd better get started, so we can get you out of here. How long ...?" I let the question hang because I couldn't quite find the right words to end it. *How long do you think you'll live?* seemed ... harsh, at best.

"As long as I can," came the simple response.

I stood and retrieved my staff. "Then I'll be as quick as I can."

Because how hard could it be to find two embattled Crones and their protectors somewhere in a network of energy lines that crisscrossed the entire planet, right? My gaze fell on the bucket, and an idea occurred to me.

I leaned across the Earth Crone and directed the light of my flame onto the wall. Immediately, I saw the spot Elysabeth had mentioned: a crack in the stone that oozed tiny drops of water marked by a dark trail below it. I couldn't see where the trail disappeared to, and a moment of doubt gripped me. Do this wrong, and the water might fill the cell—or I might accidentally seal the fissure altogether. Either way, Elysabeth would be dead within days. Do nothing, and ...

I looked down at the Earth Crone. Exhausted by our exchange, she watched me through eyes half-closed, and I knew I had no choice. She might last a few days more without food, but she needed far more than a few drops of water if she were going to survive until I returned. The question was, did I call on Water for greater flow, or on Earth to widen the crack? Goddess knew my touch with either element was anything but subtle. Just ask the house.

The staff in my grip gave a sudden twitch, and I glanced over to find it sprouting a twig just above my hand. I almost dropped it on Elysabeth in my surprise, and then I remembered its origins. I might have come to rely on it as a physical weapon, but it had been carved from the same tree that had sprung from my linden wand on the night of the attack. A tree that had likely saved my life, first by letting me out of the cupboard Keven had locked me in, and then by protecting me from the fire pixies.

And apparently one that continued to have a mind of its own.

The twig grew longer, reaching toward the wall in the same way its parent tree had sent finger-like branches into the crevices around the cupboard door so it could rip it from its frame. I tipped the staff nearer. The twig's tip prodded the length of the crack, found the spot it sought, and slipped inside. Then it began to swell.

"Not too much," I murmured. The newly formed leaves along the twig's length trembled in reply. Long seconds ticked by, and my arm holding the flame grew heavy again. I set my jaw and fought the cramp building in my bicep. Another minute, and—

A loud crack echoed through the cell. Elysabeth flinched in the bed below me, and I stopped breathing. The staff went still, then slowly the twig began to shrink back until it was once again a nub protruding just above my grip. On the wall, tiny beads of water gathered together to form a larger drop that, in turn, became a steady drip, then a trickle. I'd done it. Well. The staff had, anyway. I'd just held it ... and felt oddly disconnected from it, when I thought about it.

Elysabeth twisted around and pressed her lips to the wall, sucking greedily. I touched her shoulder with my staff hand. "Slowly," I warned. "Too much at once will make you sick."

I didn't think she'd heard me, but after a second, she nodded and sank back onto the bed, her free hand resting so that her fingers remained in the trickle, as if she were afraid it might disappear.

"I'll be careful," she whispered. "Now go."

I hesitated a moment more, looking down at her frail, shivering form. If I'd been wearing my cloak in the garden, I could have given it to her, wrapped it around her, offered her at least that much comfort. But I hadn't, and—

"Go," she said again.

Over where the ley line had spat me out onto the stone floor, a thin, pale glow emerged in the air and began a slow, writhing dance across the cell. I gave Elysabeth's skeletal shoulder a gentle press and walked across to step back into the ley.

CHAPTER 19

WHEN THE LEY SPAT ME OUT INTO THE DARK ONTO MY hands and knees for the second time, I vomited, gloriously and profusely, until I could vomit no more. Then I rested, still on all fours, with my head sagging and arms trembling from the effort of holding me above the mess I knew I'd made on the floor, though I couldn't see it.

Every fiber of my body felt like it had been violated. My bones ached, my joints were on fire, my innards had been tied in a thousand knots—even my teeth and fingernails hurt. I wouldn't have been surprised to find my skin had been flayed from me, and indeed, was rather surprised it had not.

When I was sure I wouldn't—or perhaps couldn't—throw up anymore, I pushed back until I sat on my heels, trying to get my bearings. But the dark here was as intense as it had been in the cell, and—

And what if I'm still there?

My still-fragile insides shrank from the possibility, and my tongue turned to bitter dust in my mouth. I dug my fingers into my thighs, holding myself together. No. No, this wasn't the cell. The stench of that place still clung to me, but—I took a cautious sniff of the air, testing it. But apart from that, this place smelled clean. Familiar.

I sniffed again, picking out individual scents. Herbs. Old books. The faint, damp mustiness that came with places carved from the earth. I sifted through my olfactory memories until the right one surfaced. Of course. The cellar. I'd landed in the cellar of the Earth house. No wonder it smelled familiar. Goddess knew I'd spent enough hours down here, first with Keven and lately with Anne, trying and trying and trying again to learn what didn't want to be learned by me.

131

What I hadn't been able to call on to save Elysabeth.

Elysabeth.

Lucan's Earth Crone, who was still in that putrid place, waiting for me to bring help. To bring Lucan and the others. To *find* Lucan and the others. Which meant I needed to get up off the floor and find the stairs and—

Light, I thought. *I need light.*

I loosened my grip on one thigh and lifted one hand. Or tried to. It was like lifting a boulder, it weighed so much. I settled for turning it over in my lap so that my palm faced up, and then reached into myself for the heat at my core.

It wasn't there.

I blinked into the darkness, staring down at where my hand rested, though I couldn't see it. What the—

I reached again, deeper this time, and then shivered. How had I not noticed the cold? I was *so* cold. A frisson of foreboding ran down my spine. Where was my heat? The ever-looming sense of an impending hot flash? Panic licked through me. Dear goddess, had there been something in the cell—some magick of Morok's—that had sapped my connection to Fire the way it had Elysabeth's to Earth? Was that why I'd had trouble connecting to the heat there? It had already been less, but I hadn't thought—and now it was—

"Shit, shit, shit," muttered my Claire-voice, which never swore.

"Not helping," I growled at it. Striving for calm, I inhaled a deep breath through my nose—goddess, I stank—and exhaled through my mouth. It was most likely just sheer exhaustion, I told myself. Ley travel was harder than I'd dreamed it might be, and it took a definite toll. But connection or no, I *could* still travel, and right now, that was the only magick I needed to find the others. The rest would come back later, when I stopped being disassembled.

I hoped.

But first, for now, I needed to get upstairs and get help. Help to find the help, so to speak. I giggled at my own thoughts and then clamped a lid on them, blaming fatigue. Stress. Shock. All of the above. I coaxed my brain into a more helpful mode, then giggled again because it would be helpful to find the help to find—

Oh dear goddess, Claire, stop, I told myself. I scrunched my eyes shut and pressed the heels of my hands against them. A wall. If I couldn't make light, I could just find a wall and follow it around the room until it met the stairs. See? Even with an addled brain, I could be brilliant. Or at least semi-coherent.

Elysabeth, I reminded myself. *Focus on Elysabeth*. I stretched my arms out on either side of me, as far as I could reach, but encountered nothing. Then I felt around the floor, careful to avoid the puddle I knew lay before me. If my staff had made the return trip with me—ah! There it was. My fingers closed around the familiar wooden shaft, the twelve-year-old in me sniggered at the word *shaft*, and I swore.

"For *fucksake*."

My inner adolescent withdrew in injured silence. Better. Much better. I shifted my grip on the staff, holding it at one end so I could use it as a probe. I poked it into the dark, starting on my left-hand side and working in a clockwise circle. Nothing, nothing, nothing, noth—*clunk*.

Of course, the nearest wall *would* have to be straight ahead of me, on the other side of the puddle I'd created on the floor. I sighed, grimaced, and then, using the staff as a support, hauled myself upright. My knees creaked and groaned, feeling every one of their sixty years—especially after landing twice on stone—and the effort left me panting, but I made it, and holy hell, but ley travel was hard on a body.

It took a few minutes, a bruised shin, and more cursing—and I was fairly certain that if I'd gone in the other direction, I would have reached my target already—but I finally groped my way around the cellar to the stairs that led up and out. I paused at their base to attempt conjuring light again, but my core remained cold and unresponsive, so I tucked my staff under one arm and did the only thing I could: I crawled up on my hands and highly indignant knees.

As I traveled, keeping my shoulder snug against the wall to my right so I didn't slip off the open edge of the stairs and plummet back into the cellar, I wrestled with what I'd do when I got to the top. More precisely, who I'd go to with my discovery and haphazard plan.

I considered the options. Anne would likely insist on coming with me, but she was in no shape to do so. My non-magickal family, Natalie's apparent potion prowess aside, was also out, as was Keven, whose knowledge was limited to this house.

That left—

Oh goddess, no. I cringed from the idea. Surely there was another way. There *had* to be another way. But there were only so many people in the house, and like it or not, I'd run out of names. Like it or not, there was only one person who could help me right now—and I suspected he'd be as amenable to my request as I was to making it.

"Fuckity fuck fuck—ow!" My head connected with the solid oak door at the top of the stairs. I hadn't even noticed I'd hit the little landing. I gave the emerging lump on my skull a perfunctory rub as I struggled to my feet again. I was *not* looking forward to this.

But Elysabeth.

I pulled the tatters of my resolve around me like a worn-out cloak, felt around until I found the doorknob, and thrust open the cellar door. Of all the people I didn't want to need, it had to be—

Bedivere emerged from the kitchen and stopped short.

"You," I said.

His scowl at seeing me rivaled my own, and his gaze raked over me from head to toe. "What about me?" Before I could answer, his nostrils flared and he stepped toward me, close enough that I could feel the heat radiating from him. He sniffed at my shoulder. His scowl became a glower. "Where have you been? You smell like—"

Over his shoulder, I saw Keven's head turn toward us and, and behind her, Natalie's. Without thinking, I slapped a hand over Bedivere's mouth to stop his words. I'm not sure which one of us was more surprised, but Bedivere was certainly first to react.

In less than the blink of an eye, he morphed into his wolf form and lunged up from the floor at me. A stone fist caught him by the scruff of the neck in mid-air and held him away, snarling and twisting. I pressed myself flat against the wall, my heart doing a tap dance à la Ginger Rogers in my throat, and stared at the slavering jaws that had only just missed their target. If I hadn't already thrown up everything in my stomach and then some, I was pretty sure I would have been heaving again.

"Do you have a death wish?" Keven demanded of me, her granite expression managing to convey both annoyance and astonishment at the same time. Then, not waiting for an answer —likely because she thought it obvious and, after the stunt I'd just pulled, I rather concurred—she shook Bedivere and growled, "Enough. Like it or not, Lady Claire is still Crone, so pull yourself together."

She dropped him to the floor, thumped him on the head with one finger for emphasis, and planted her hands on her haunches as she waited for him to return to his human self. He did, but I wasn't at all certain it made him any less threatening. Keven, however, grunted approval, ordered, "Get dressed and join us," and then seized my arm above the elbow and herded me ahead of her into the kitchen.

Natalie, who had been watching open-mouthed with a steaming pot in hand, scurried out of the way, and the gargoyle pushed me onto one of the benches running the length of the table.

"Are you okay?" my daughter-in-law mouthed.

I was about as far from okay as I could be, but my heart had returned to its rightful place if not its usual steady beat, so I nodded. Keven went to the wood stove and moved a pot of water onto the heat, then took down a selection of herbs from the shelves. I didn't want or have time for tea, but I wisely kept silent, looking away as a glowering Bedivere entered, tucking his shirt into his unbuttoned trousers.

"Right," the gargoyle said. "What was it you didn't want me to hear?"

I hesitated. I'd wanted to do this without a lot of fanfare, and without the objections I knew would be raised, because I didn't have time for arguments. Elysabeth didn't have time.

Keven waved a spoon at me. "You're not leaving this kitchen until you tell me what's going on, milady, beginning with why you abandoned my basket of herbs in the garden and how you got into the cellar without me seeing you come in."

Bedivere's expression turned even more sour at the way she addressed me, but he looked as if he might back her up on the threat, and I sighed.

"Do you want me to leave?" Natalie asked. I considered the offer, then shook my head. If I didn't come back, she and Paul should at least know what had happened to me.

"No, you can stay," I said, and then I met Keven's implacable gaze. I might have had a slim chance of convincing Bedivere to stay quiet for the sake of his Crone's safety, but Keven? Not a chance. I heaved a sigh, laid my staff on the bench beside me, and folded my arms on the table before me. "We may as well get Lady Anne in here, too," I said. "Because I've found the Earth Crone."

"*Wait—you* what *now?*" Edie demanded.

It was about bloody time she turned up again—but why did she sound like she was at the bottom of a barrel?

"I DON'T BELIEVE YOU," BEDIVERE SAID WHEN I FINISHED my tale, his voice as flat as his gaze was sharp—and twice as suspicious.

He hovered behind Anne, where I could see his expression, but she couldn't. She stared down at the worn tabletop, tracing the grain with one fingertip, and I suspected she didn't much believe me, either. Although, to be fair, my story had sounded pretty fantastical even to my own ears.

I glanced over at Keven, who had kept her back to me as she went about dinner preparations. "I know it sounds far-fetched," I said, inwardly appealing to her to back me up. Of all the people present, she at least knew what I was capable of. Sometimes. "But—"

The gargoyle cut me off. "Crones cannot travel the ley alone," she said, her voice as flat as Bedivere's had been as she continued to chop onions.

Sudden impatience, fueled by urgency, flared in me. "Crones can't call on all four elements, either," I replied tartly. "And yet, here we are."

"Ooh," said Edie. "Nice one."

She still sounded distant, muffled, and I stuck a finger in my ear and wiggled it around as the gargoyle looked over her shoulder at me in surprise. It occurred to me that this was the first time I'd stood up for myself with Keven. The first time I'd voluntarily laid claim to my powers. I processed my surprise, hiding it in the act of cleaning out my other ear as Anne continued to stare down at the tabletop in silence. Across the kitchen, the gargoyle exchanged a look with Bedivere that annoyed me as much as the looks she used to share with Lucan.

Used to, because Lucan hadn't miraculously returned in my absence.

Lucan, who hadn't been at the end of the ley I'd traveled, but whose scent—and unmistakable presence—had still somehow led me to Elysabeth. As if she were already marked by her bond with him, even though they had yet to meet. Something tight-

LYDIA M. HAWKE

ened in my chest at the thought, but I turned away from it. I had neither the time nor the energy to spend on navel-gazing right now. Not with two other Crones to find. Which brought me back to the point of this whole conversation-slash-confrontation.

I girded my mental loins, curled the fingernails of one hand into my palm, and reached the other out to touch Anne's. She lifted her gaze to mine.

"I need Bedivere's help," I said. "I need him to—"

The shifter's derisive snort interrupted me. "*My* help."

I continued speaking to Anne. Bedivere took his orders from her, and she was the one I had to convince. "I need him to show me the ley line that Lucan followed, so that I can go after him and the others."

This time, Bedivere outright laughed. "You. On your own."

"Unless you're willing to come with me," I responded tartly, safe in the knowledge that he would never leave Anne, "then yes. Me. On my own."

He crossed his arms. "No."

I ignored him. Bedivere ignored that I was ignoring him.

"In case I haven't mentioned it, *milady*," he said, "I don't trust you. I've seen the results of Morok's treachery too many times."

That got my attention.

"Excuse me?" I gaped at him. "You seriously think I'm working for Morok?"

"Perhaps not directly," Bedivere allowed, looking down his nose at me. "But some are easily led by the god of lies and deceit. The Mages are here for a reason. They have targeted your family for a reason. There is something about you—"

"They fear her," Keven said, rhythmically slicing carrots at the counter, her back to us. "You weren't here when the goliath attacked. You didn't see her power."

Oh, so *now* she'd back me up.

Bedivere snorted. "If they're so afraid, why did they come

138

back? Why don't they just stay away, instead of setting up such an obvious presence?"

Keven's slicing slowed. She had no response.

Anne rose from the bench and slowly paced the room. Each step brought a wince, along with a deepening of Bedivere's concern. Our morning lesson had tired her today, and he slanted me a malevolent glare filled with blame. I looked away.

At the far end of the table, a silent Natalie tied the herbs I'd cut earlier into bundles for drying. On the floor by the back door, Braden played with the pink-flowered dolls, an indifferent Gus loafing beside him. Only Paul remained missing from our company, and I gritted my teeth. I was fast losing patience with my petulant son, and—

"One problem at a time," Edie counseled faintly as I began to rise.

I planted my butt back on the bench. I didn't know what was wrong with my friend's voice, but yes. Elysabeth first.

Anne stopped walking and leaned on her stick. She turned her attention to her shifter.

"I think you and the gargoyle are both right, Bedivere," she said. "Your point is valid about the Mages not coming after Claire's family again despite their obvious presence, but so is the gargoyle's about them being afraid of her. Or at least uncertain about her. I think their presence is designed to make sure Claire's focus remains here, with her family and the house. That *she* remains here. They're keeping her distracted."

I waited for a sense of validation, because that was the exact conclusion I'd reached earlier in the garden, but all I felt was nauseous—and still cold. So very much rode on my supposed powers. "If Morok gets Elysabeth's pendant ..."

Anne compressed her lips in a thin line. "If he gets any of them," she said, "Elysabeth is right. We are finished." She resumed pacing, walking to the wood stove and then back again before stopping beside me. "If you and I go to her together, perhaps we might—"

"Absolutely *not*," snarled her protector.

Anne lifted her chin and stared down her nose at him. "Let us remember which one of us is in charge, Bedivere. If I decide—"

"Let us also remember which one of us is driven to protect the other," he retorted. "Even if I thought you were right to try —which I don't—my bond wouldn't let me. Not while you're still so far from healed."

Anne's shoulders sagged, and she leaned again on her walking stick. "Fine." She sighed and faced me again. "Bedivere will show you the line, but are you sure you want to do this? If we're mistaken ..."

"Milady," Bedivere growled, but Anne lifted a single finger on the hand clutching the walking stick, and he fell silent. Word-wise, anyway. Expression-wise, it was a whole other story, and his taut features spoke volumes. So did the grim doubt written across Keven's granite face.

I looked to my grandson, playing on the floor, oblivious to the discussion taking place around him. The ramifications that discussion could have. Was I sure about this? Not at all. Because if we *were* wrong, I would be leaving this house vulnerable— and, with it, my family. Even if the Mages didn't attack, there remained a chance I might not return from whatever the ley line carried me into. That I would remain cold at my core and not be able to access my magick ... or that I would, but I would be no match for what I found ...

Or that I would unleash another disaster.

I shuddered at all the possibilities, most of which I didn't dare think about, lest I change my mind. Because while I might not be sure about any of it, neither did I have a choice. Elysabeth's time was running out, and with it, everyone else's.

I turned my gaze to Bedivere. "I'll meet you out front in ten minutes," I said.

Right after I had a little chat with my son—because, Edie's point aside, he was out of time, too.

CHAPTER 20

I BARGED INTO PAUL AND NATALIE'S ROOM WITHOUT knocking, not giving myself time to reconsider the idea. I was done second guessing myself. I'd spent an entire lifetime doing that, and I'd decided I didn't much like what I had to show for it. Specifically, a life spent giving in to others, a divorce, and a spoiled, privileged son who'd turned out entirely too much like his spoiled, privileged father.

Paul sat slouched in a chair by the fireplace, still in the pajamas and robe the midwitches had packed for him when they'd brought him to the house. His expression turned surly when he saw me. "I don't want—" he began, but I didn't let him finish.

"Grow up," I snapped.

His unshaven jaw dropped. "I beg your pardon!"

"As you should." I stalked across the room and used my staff to shove the footstool out from under his feet. "You've behaved like a spoiled brat since you arrived, Paul Emerson, and—"

"Since I was *kidnapped*, you mean."

"Since you were brought here for your own safety," I corrected, crossing my arms and returning glare for glare. "And you are more than welcome to leave at any time. What you are *not* welcome to do is continue sulking in this room while my gargoyle and your wife wait on you hand and foot."

The very mention of Keven—who wasn't mine, but semantics—made him hunch further into the chair, his chin drawn into his chest. "*Gargoyle*," he muttered. "Have you any idea how bizarre that sounds?"

"I do. And again, I don't care. Things are different here. No one gets that more than I do, believe me. But you need to find a way to deal with it, and if you can't, you seriously need to leave."

"You know I won't go without Nat and Braden."

"I also know you're not currently *with* Nat and Braden, either."

He sent me a dark look. "My marriage is none of—"

"Oh, please. Do you really want to travel the same path as your father? Because that's exactly where you're headed, child of mine. I spent a lifetime catering to that man's every whim, remember?"

"I don't expect Natalie to cater to me."

"And yet here you are." I waved my hand at the room, encompassing the rumpled, unmade bed, the half-drawn curtains, and his appearance. "The only difference I see in your marriage is that your wife is better than I was at maintaining her own person—and that she has less patience than I had."

He snorted. "This is you being patient?"

"This is me now," I said. "And I'm out of patience."

"You're certainly different from what you used to be, I'll give you that," he muttered. "I feel like I don't even know you anymore."

Well, you won't get to know me by sitting in here, I thought, but I kept the comment to myself, because even without a watch, I knew my ten minutes were up. Bedivere would be waiting for me.

"I have to leave," I said. "Your wife and son are in the kitchen. Get dressed. Shave. Go downstairs. Make yourself useful."

"I—wait—what do you mean, leave?" He struggled upright in the chair as I turned toward the door. "Leave where? And for how long? I thought you said it wasn't safe to go anywhere."

"It's not." I didn't sugar-coat my reply. There was no point, not when Natalie would fill him in on the plan as soon as I left. One hand on the doorframe, I looked back at him. "I need you to step up, Paul. I don't think anyone will come after you when I'm gone, but if they do, you need to be ready. Look after your family. Listen to Lady Anne and Bedivere and Keven, and whatever they tell you to do, do it. Without question. Do you understand?"

He slumped back in the chair again and scrubbed both hands over his several-days-old shadow. "I don't understand any of this," he grumbled, the petulance returning. "And I'm not taking orders from anyone, least of all you."

I had a sudden urge to go back into the room and whack my darling son upside the head, but again ... time. I would have to leave it to Natalie to talk sense to him and hope she would have more success than I'd had. Sadly, I shook my head at him.

"I'm sorry," I said.

"For what? Bringing us here? Putting us in danger with all this weird shit you have going on?"

"Honestly? For not grounding you more often when I had the chance," I replied. Leaving the door open, I turned my back on my only offspring's outrage and strode down the corridor toward my purpose. My last thought about him was that Edie had been right. She totally should have handed out more detentions to him, too.

"*Told you,*" my friend whispered.

NATALIE STOOD AT THE BOTTOM OF THE STAIRS, MY DARK blue cloak draped over one arm as she watched me descend. "How did it go? Or should I even ask?"

I shook my head and leaned my staff against the stair post, where a suit of armor had once stood until I destroyed it along with so many other things. Even though the house had mostly repaired itself, the armor hadn't been replaced, and I hadn't been able to bring myself to ask about it.

Natalie sighed and handed over the cloak. I accepted it from her in silence, part of me wishing I'd had it when I'd gone to Elysabeth so I could have left it with her. But it would be good to have it with me now, too, especially since I had no idea where the ley would take me. If it was cold, the garment would keep me warm; if it was hot, it would keep me cool. That part of magick, I rather liked.

That part.

I draped the cloak around my shoulders and fastened it at my throat, grateful for its warmth because goddess, it was cold without the heat at my core. I took my staff in hand again and turned to my daughter-in-law. "Natalie, if I don't—"

"Shh." She put a finger over my lips, her eyes glistening. "I don't even want to hear it."

I pulled her in for a hug, this surprisingly fierce creature whom I'd underestimated all these years. When all of this was behind us—if it ever was—I would apologize to her for that, and for all the petty little judgments I'd made.

And for my son, damn his spoiled hide.

I pulled back, and Natalie released me with reluctance.

"I do love him, you know," I said.

She smiled through her tears. "So do I," she assured me. "And I'll tell him that. Right after I box his ears for you."

I couldn't quite laugh, but I managed a return smile. Then I gazed for a moment down the corridor in the direction of the kitchen and Keven and Braden, aching to go to them, to say goodbye and hold Braden and feel Gus's softness beneath my hand one last time. To ask Keven to believe in me at least a little.

"You've got this, Maman," Natalie whispered. "I trust you."

My throat went tight, and my eyes flooded with tears. I blinked them back and then, unable to look at her again, let alone respond, I half-walked, half-stumbled across the entry to the front door. I fumbled for the knob, twisted it, and pulled open the heavy oak—perhaps for the last time ever.

I was glad one of us trusted me, because, goddess, I so did *not* have this.

Anne waited for me on the front porch. I took a deep breath as I closed the door on my family and Keven and the house, then turned to her, making no effort to hide my emotions. I was pretty sure I couldn't have hidden them if I'd tried. What I undertook might be necessary, but it was also hard, and I could see from the soft compassion behind her concern that she understood that. I could also see that her concern was uppermost.

"You can still change your mind," she said, her grip on her walking stick as white-knuckled as mine on my staff. "We can try to find another way."

"We both know there is no other way, Anne," I said. "Elysabeth won't last much longer, someone has to find the others, and you're not healed enough to do it yourself."

"And you're sure ..." She trailed off and looked away, as doubt joined concern.

You're sure you can do this. You're sure you won't lose control and make things worse.

Even unspoken, the words sat heavy between us, weighing down our farewell. I hesitated, wondering for a moment if it would help to tell her I couldn't lose control of what I could no longer connect with, and deciding it wouldn't. Instead, I tightened my hold on the staff until my fingers ached and I wasn't sure I could unlock them again, and I told a different truth.

"I'm sure I have to try," I said simply.

Acknowledgment flared in her brown eyes, and she nodded.

"And you?" I asked. "You can ..." It was my turn to trail off as I glanced at the house with my family inside.

"I will do everything I can," she said. "And I've sent a message to Kate to let her and the midwitches know what's happening. I've asked her to stay here until your return."

"Won't that impact our groups of five?"

She turned her gaze away from me and toward the trees, but not before I saw the weariness and worry in it. "Be careful," she said, by way of an answer that wasn't an answer, "and goddess speed. Bedivere is waiting for you at the side of the house."

I hesitated, but I could think of nothing more to say. There *was* nothing more. I knew she would do the best she could here; she knew I would do the best I could wherever the ley took me. No more could be asked of either of us.

"Except perhaps the truth about your magick," my Claire-voice said with a disapproving sniff.

But my Claire-voice was wrong, I told myself. The truth about my magick would only bring Anne more uncertainty and worry, neither of which she needed when she already carried so much. So I put a hand over the Water Crone's on her walking stick and gave her fingers a squeeze. "I'll be as fast as I can," I promised. Then I stepped down onto the grass and started in search of Bedivere.

Edie joined me as I neared the corner of the house. *"Anne is —are you—about this?"*

Her voice faded in and out, dropping half her words, and my step slowed. "What's wrong with your voice?" I asked. "You sound like we have a bad connection."

She snorted, sounding like static. *"Good analogy. I'm— trouble reaching—veil—weird. Something—off—you."*

I frowned, trying to decipher her broken words. Something off...something was off about me? I was the issue? Did that mean Edie could sense—I caught my breath as ice crystals formed in my already-cold core.

"Sense what?"

I hesitated. Should I explain what I suspected? My doubts loomed anew, and I snapped my mind shut against them— against what I'd told no one.

"Wait. What haven't—told—"

Gosh, but the autumn colors were pretty this year. I picked up my pace and rounded the corner.

"Claire Emer—" Even muffled and static-y, Edie's voice took on the high school principal tone. *"What—hiding?"*

Only that I'd lost—no. I began humming the tune of "Ninety-Nine Bottles of Beer" under my breath, focusing my gaze on Bedivere, who waited in the middle of the side clearing. I didn't want to put it into words. Saying it would make it real. Might make it—

The linden staff jerked out of my hand, flipped horizontal, and hovered in midair at nose height, blocking my path. Edie's teapot trick. On steroids.

"Damn it, Edie, stop that," I hissed. I shot a look at the scowling shifter, whose sudden tension showed in every watchful line of his body. "Bedivere is watching, for heaven's sake."

"—*don't care. You're not—another step—come clean. What the —going on? What—lost?*"

I wrapped my cloak tighter around me against the inner cold and stared at the staff, my resolve wavering. What was going on was big, I thought. Bigger by far than I wanted to handle alone. But what would be the point in telling her? She couldn't fix it. Couldn't undo it. Could do nothing but worry.

"*Friends—worry. It's—job.*"

I raised my gaze past the staff to Bedivere again. Saw him start toward us—me. The staff wobbled. I was losing her. I was losing Edie, my last...my only friend. If I was right about the toll that ley travel took on me—

"—*aire Emers—!*"

"What the *fuck* is that?" Bedivere stopped a half-dozen feet away and pointed his only hand at the floating staff.

I plucked the staff from the air. I met no resistance. Heard no objection. Couldn't even hear any static. Edie was gone again, and if I was right, then by the time I returned with the others —*if* I returned—she would be gone for good.

And with that, my decision was made for me.

"It's nothing," I told Bedivere. "I'm ready."

The shifter crossed his arms and glared at me. "And I'm not showing you a thing until you explain—"

But I was in no mood to listen to his objections again.

"Oh, for the goddess's sake, Bedivere, stuff it," I said, heaving a weary sigh. I'd had my fill of the men in my life telling me what not to do—and as I'd known Bedivere for a scant week, he didn't even qualify as such a man. "You've made your position clear. I know you don't approve of me or my plan, but what else would you have us do? Sit here like ducks, waiting for the hunters to arrive?"

The shifter's jaw tightened, and for a moment, I thought he might refuse to help after all. But Lady Anne's orders won out.

"The line you need crosses the garden," he growled. He stomped off toward the back of the house, leaving me to scurry after him and, when we arrived at the garden, to awkwardly clamber over the fence in his wake. He offered no assistance, and I wasn't sure I would have accepted if he had.

He waited for me in the same spot I'd stood when I'd first seen the ley that took me to Elysabeth, and as I stepped over a hill of potatoes to join him, my stomach did a queasy roll at the thought of what was coming. I really wasn't looking forward to a repeat of my travel experience.

"There," he said, pointing.

My gaze followed the direction of his finger. At first, I saw nothing. Then a faint, wavering ribbon of light took shape. It was the same pastel rainbow of color that the first had been, and it moved in the same undulating fashion. I traced its path into the trees. Blinked. Blinked again.

It didn't just look the same. It *was* the same. Literally.

I gaped at Bedivere. "But—that's the one that took me to Elysabeth!"

Bedivere stared into the woods. "You're sure?"

I gathered my cloak and lifted it clear of my ankles, then stepped over a low hedge of lavender, closer to the ley. I leaned in and breathed. Lucan's scent filled my nostrils, and his presence reached out to meet mine. I clung to it for a moment, then stepped back and straightened. "I'm positive."

Behind me, the shifter grunted, but whether in surprise or

disbelief, I couldn't be sure. Then a hand settled onto my shoulder and turned me away from the woods and toward the house, into which the other end of the ribbon disappeared. "Lucan went that way."

Surprise prickled along my skin. So I really had sensed him in the ley. I'd just gone in the wrong direction—or the right one, if I believed in divine intervention. Which, after two encounters with the Morrigan, I felt I must—at least a little.

I took a deep breath, held it a second, then released it in a gust. "Right then. That's the way I'll go, too."

But Bedivere's hand tightened on my shoulder, stopping me from stepping forward. I looked back at him, raising an eyebrow. His gaze traveled over me from head to toe and back again, as it often had, but this time the expression behind it was different. Less hostile. More speculative. Perhaps even a bit curious.

"You really traveled the ley," he said. "Alone."

I gave a snort of laughter. "Travel might be a bit of a misnomer, but yes. I did."

"How did you survive?"

I thought of how I had been torn limb from limb in the ribbon of light. Remembered how I had been shredded and dissolved and then reassembled and spat out at my destination. Relived, for the nanosecond before my brain shied away from the memory, the agony that had overwhelmed me—that had *been* me. Shivered at the ice crystals at my center, where my heat no longer sat.

Felt, keenly, the absence of my friend.

Then, as I stared at the ley I was about to travel again—voluntarily, no less—I spoke the truth.

"I'm not sure I did survive," I answered Bedivere.

I moved out from under his hand and into the shimmering light. I thought I heard a quiet *"Good luck, milady,"* as the cold swallowed me, but from Bedivere? Impossible.

I decided I had imagined it—and then I became agony.

CHAPTER 21

JUST BECAUSE I *COULD* TRAVEL THE LEY DIDN'T MEAN I should. Especially twice, back-to-back the way I just had.

I lay curled in a ball of misery, the surface beneath me hard and unforgiving, waiting for my body to knit itself back together again. Or at least to be able to open my eyes without a wave of vertigo bringing a fresh round of retching. I squeezed said eyes tighter as my stomach rolled uneasily.

The ley Bedivere had shown me had taken me to the destroyed Water house as he'd said it would. As I'd expected, I found neither Lucan nor the others there. I'd begun my search for him as soon as I had my feet back under me, but the ruins of the house had been lit up from one end to the other by ley lines that ran in every direction, glowing and writhing, and Lucan's scent—his presence—had been in every one of them.

I'd staggered from one to another and back again, checking and re-checking, trying to find the one where my sense of him seemed strongest. I'd finally narrowed it down to two, and then, because I'd had to make a final decision, I'd closed my eyes and stepped into the one that brought me here, hoping I wouldn't have to backtrack and take the other.

Not sure I would have the strength left to try.

I had no idea where the line had brought me—or whether it had dropped me inside or out, or how long I'd lain here, or what danger lurked in the vicinity. I could have been in the middle of Morok's lair itself, and I didn't think I would have cared.

The possibility made me crack open one eye. Well. Maybe I cared a little.

The world around me wobbled, then settled into place. Indoors, I decided, as I peered at my shadowed surroundings. I'd definitely landed indoors—which, unfortunately, didn't remove the possibility that this was Morok's lair.

With my nausea receding, my sense of self-preservation began to resurface. Lair or otherwise, I couldn't stay here forever. I held my breath, straining to listen for movement, voices, anything that might give me a hint as to my whereabouts. But the silence in the room was complete. Muffled. Tomblike, if I were honest. Wherever I was, I was alone.

Cautiously, I opened my other eye and waited for it to coordinate with its mate and adjust to the near dark, then I began picking out what features I could in the shadows. The floor beneath my cheek, befouled by the remnants of the tea Keven had given me, was wood. A couple of yards away, I could see what looked like a table leg, and beside that, an overturned chair.

It appeared I'd landed in a dining room. Or at least, the remains of one.

Because the chair in the shadows wasn't just overturned, it had been smashed to pieces—as had its companions, and the massive table that had once dominated the space. Wallpaper hung in tatters, and—I squinted harder at the dark far corner. Was that ...?

Dear goddess, it was a pair of boots. I jolted upright, fear a hard tangle in my throat. The room tilted and my stomach heaved.

So much for being alone.

I squeezed my lips and eyes shut, counted to three in my head, and tried again. This time, things stayed where they belonged, and I peered into the gloom. Overhead, a chandelier flickered weakly, enough so I could see that the boots hadn't moved and that they were prone, rather than upright. They also had unmistakable legs protruding from them. The lump returned to my throat, this time for a different reason.

Lucan.

I struggled to my feet, swayed, used my staff to find my

balance. A frisson of unease wound through me. The first trip in the ley had hurt like hell, but I'd still had all my faculties when I'd landed in Elysabeth's cell. The second trip had left me on all fours and spectacularly sick all over the floor of the cellar, but still able to stand up and move almost normally after a few minutes. The third one to the Water house, followed so closely by this fourth one, however ...

I put away the nagging worry that I might have over-stretched and shuffled forward, acutely aware of the noise my feet made against the wood floor but incapable of lifting them just yet.

I halted a few feet and two broken chairs away from the boots. They remained motionless, and I let out a small hiss of relief because my bones still thrummed with remembered agony, and it was all I could do to stay upright, even with the staff's help. If the feet had belonged to a threat, I would have been toast, unable to run to save my own life, or to lift the staff from the floor without falling over.

Or to call on the slightest magick in my defense.

I tested my hypothesis by holding out an experimental palm, because I could have used more light in the darkened room. But my arm trembled, I produced no flame, and the insidious cold at my core felt like it had formed ice crystals.

I let my hand fall back to my side and steeled myself. Magick or no magick, I'd made this trip for a reason, and I couldn't put off knowing any longer.

My gaze found the boots on the floor again and traveled along them to the pant legs that emerged at their tops. Jeans. I sagged in relief. It wasn't Lucan. Thank the goddess. But if not him, then who?

With the chandelier continuing its sporadic efforts, I scuffed a few feet closer for a better look. A flicker illuminated a narrow leather belt with an oversized buckle bearing an ornate, gothic letter "M"; another flicker, a half-untucked black shirt under a long, heavy, black coat splayed out beneath the body. More flickers as I watched the chest beneath the shirt for a few seconds. Like the feet, it didn't move.

So. Definitely a body, and one belonging to a man, so not a Crone, either. A Mage, then? My gaze flicked back to the belt buckle, and I shivered. "M" for Morok? It seemed likely.

I bent down, curious to see more of the person who would so blatantly display his affiliation with the dark god. The chandelier flickered. I leaned closer, and slowly, my eyes picked out the body's face from the shadows.

Or what should have been the face. Because everything that was supposed to be there—eyes, nose, mouth—all those features were missing, along with what should have been beneath them. Skin, bone, brains. It was all gone. Everything. Nothing remained except a bloody, hollowed-out half-skull with a seething mass of maggots at its center.

My world tipped sideways, and whatever contents remained in my stomach vaulted into my throat. I slapped my hand over my mouth against the rising gorge and turned my head, squeezing my eyes shut.

And then, through the rush of blood against my eardrums, I heard it.

The faint *click, click, click* of approaching claws on wood.

"WILL SHE BE ALL RIGHT?" A WOMAN'S VOICE ASKED FROM far away.

Another—gravelly like Keven's, but not Keven's—responded, "She'll be fine once she wakes, but she'll have a nasty bruise on her forehead."

"How in the world did she get through the wards?" murmured a third voice—another woman, and another I didn't recognize. "Surely we would have felt the breach."

"You really shouldn't have pushed her that hard, Lucan," the first woman admonished.

"You would have preferred I let your dogs take out her throat?" yet another voice growled.

I smiled inside my fluffy, cushion-y cloud. Now *that* voice I recognized. Then I frowned, remembering that Lucan wasn't here. He'd gone somewhere, and I needed to find him. Befuddlement made my thoughts heavy. Foggy. But if he wasn't here, why was I hearing him?

"She's waking up," said the gravelly voice.

A dream, I decided. I must be dreaming him—Lucan, not the voice.

Or maybe the voice, too?

I frowned again. It was all very muddled.

"What's her name again?" the first woman asked.

"Claire," said Lucan. His voice was closer, and I let my frown slide away as my smile returned. Muddled or not, I liked dreaming him. "Her name is Lady Claire."

And I especially liked how my name sounded when he— wait. Why had he said my name? Were they talking about *me*? Maybe this wasn't a dream. But then, why could I hear them and not see them? I couldn't see anything, now that I thought about it. Why was it so dark? Goddess, maybe this was another nightmare. I hated nightmares.

"Milady?" Lucan said. "Can you open your eyes?"

A warm hand brushed against my brow, and I winced. The gravelly voice had been right about the bruise, and if that was real, then this was no dream, and they were definitely talking about me. But it was so dark. How could they see me in the—

"Lady Claire, open your eyes," Lucan said.

Eyes—of course. That explained it. I took a deep breath and swam my way up and out of the cotton cloud, blinking as I emerged into the light. The warm hand stroked my cheek, and I turned toward the touch. Lucan's face hovered near mine, haggard and worn as he crouched beside me. His amber eyes were dark with concern.

"Hey," I croaked, trying to dig my smile out of my dream and bring it into real life. "Fancy meeting you here."

The concern remained, but an answering smile tugged at the corner of his mouth beneath the beard. "I've only been here for a couple of hours," he said. "The question is, what are *you* doing here?"

I pursed my lips and frowned. Good question. I tried to remember. "I know I was looking for you," I murmured, "but—"

Something moved in my peripheral vision, and for the breath of an instant, my brain froze. Then it exploded into a tumult of terror mixed with sudden flashes of images. Now I remembered. A hollow head missing ... everything. Maggots spilling from it onto the floor. Nails clicking across a wood floor. A wolf leaping for my throat. Another wolf knocking me aside at the last instant, its teeth meeting the other wolf's with a grinding clash, the memory of which jarred afresh down my spine.

I lunged to my feet and instinctively, mindlessly, reached inside myself for my magick. Emptiness greeted me. No hint of power, no connection, no—

"Milady, it's all right. You're safe." Lucan's arms went around me. I fought him, but only for an instant—because it was all the fight I had left in me. My limbs turned to liquid, and I collapsed against him and leaned into his shelter. His strength. His comfort.

"You're safe," he repeated.

My face buried in his chest, I took a deep, shuddering breath, then another. Lucan's heart thudded against my nose, strong and steady like the rise and fall of his breathing. I focused on those, matching my own breath to his, and the shivers wracking my body began to subside.

My brain began to function again. It had been Lucan's wolf that had knocked the other aside. I'd found Lucan. I'd found him, and he was alive, and there were others with him, which meant ... I turned my head until I could see past his chest to the little group clustered beside the fireplace, on the other side of a square, white coffee table from us. A gargoyle with a long neck and the head of a lion, a slender, bird-like body, and feathers carved along its stone wings. Two women—one tall and lean to the point of thin, gray hair cropped close to her head; the other short and heavier set, with a tumble of curls dyed a shocking red. And two men, one bearded and towering over the other, both dressed in the same loose clothing protectors favored, and both scowling at me—as protectors were wont to do.

The knot that had been in my chest since my trip to Elysabeth's cell unwound just a little. I'd found them. Crones and protectors. They were all alive, and now they could—

I pulled back and looked up at Lucan, remembering why I'd come. Remembering that Elysabeth waited for my return and her rescue. I wound fistfuls of his shirt into my hands and did a triumphant little jig that was more like a shuffle because my feet still felt like they weighed a thousand pounds each.

"I found her!" I exclaimed. "But she's in trouble—she's dying. We have to save her!"

I detached from Lucan and tottered toward the door, dragging my feet across the wood floor. I didn't relish returning to the room with the hollowed-out body, but that's where the ley line was, so there wasn't much choice. I'd gone maybe a dozen steps, however, when I got the distinct feeling I was alone in my hurry. A glance over my shoulder confirmed that no one else had moved, and I stopped and turned back. Mixed expressions of distrust on the protectors' parts and confusion on the Crones' met my indignation.

"Didn't you hear me? I found her!" I repeated.

What was wrong with these people?

"We have to save her!"

"Who?" Lucan asked. "Who did you find, milady?"

Hands on hips, I opened my mouth to repeat myself, and then snapped it shut again. Ah. I'd forgotten that part, hadn't I? "Elysabeth," I told him. I squared my shoulders and took a deep breath. "I found Lady Elysabeth, Lucan. I found your Crone."

THE REDHEADED WOMAN WAS THE FIRST TO MOVE AFTER I dropped my bombshell. She marched across the room to take my arm and steer me back to the sofa I'd vacated.

"I'm Maureen, the Air Crone," she said, pushing me down and tucking the blanket around me, ignoring my feeble attempts at protest. She pointed at the tall, thin woman standing with the protectors. "And that's Lady Nia, the Fire Crone. This is their house."

"Their?" The question slipped from me before I could think better of it. Probably because I was distracted by Nia being the Fire Crone when I'd mentally paired that element with Maureen's shocking red curls.

"I'm Trans," Nia said. "My pronouns are they and their." A simple statement, but the smile that accompanied it didn't quite reach watchful dark eyes as they waited—braced?—for my reaction.

With surprising swiftness, given its level of exhaustion, my brain processed the information, acknowledged the truth of inclusivity in the divine feminine that I served, and made note of the pronouns to be used.

"Good to know," I said to Nia, adding a nod of acknowledgement, then grabbing onto the blanket when my head swam. Maureen tutted under her breath and—despite it being Nia's house rather than her own—ordered the gargoyle to fetch tea.

"Something restorative," she added, looking down at me.

The gargoyle inclined its head and shambled out of the room. In the wake of its departure, Nia went to check the wards, along with Lucan and the tall, muscular protector they called Yvain, and Maureen put her own protector, the slightly built but wiry Percival, to work stoking the fire. She refused to hear a word from me until everyone returned, so I wrapped my cloak around my shoulders, huddled under the blanket she'd given me, and struggled to stay awake—because, goddess, I was tired.

The gargoyle returned first, setting a tray on the white-painted wood coffee table between the sofas as Nia came back into the room with Lucan and Yvain.

"Well?" Maureen asked. Nia assured her, to my relief, that the wards remained in place.

Judging by the look Lucan gave me on their return, he'd expected the same thing I had—that the wards would have fled upon my arrival. Perhaps they'd forgiven me at last, I thought. Or maybe they'd sensed what I felt: the emptiness inside me that I was trying hard to ignore, that made me feel disconnected from everything around me—including me.

I turned away from the panic I felt hovering along the edges of my brain. *Later*, I promised myself. I'd figure it out later, when I had more time. Right now ...

Right now, I tightened my grip on the mug of tea Maureen had given me. She settled herself on the slipcovered sofa at my side and half-turned to face me. I leaned against the floral chintz cushions and plucked at the blanket covering my lap as I assembled my words. And then, for the second time in the space of hours, I launched into my tale of ley travel and finding the Earth Crone. Of how she was imprisoned and on the verge of death. Of how it was imperative we save her before Morok got her pendant.

The story sounded just as fantastical the second time around as it had the first, and it met with equal disbelief.

"Not possible," Yvain announced when I finished.

Percival regarded me narrowly but refrained from comment, as did the Air and Fire Crones.

"Even if you *could* manage to connect with one of the lines —and I doubt even that's possible—you'd never survive travel on your own," Yvain continued. "Without a being of magick to absorb the energy, it would tear you apart."

It was an apt description, with an unspoken accusation behind it—because if I hadn't traveled the ley on my own, who or what had brought me? I ignored the accusation part.

"And then it reassembles me," I said, raising my gaze to his. "Yes."

At least mostly. I shivered and drew the blanket closer.

Later, I reminded myself.

Yvain stared at me. "Impossible," he said stubbornly.

Lucan cleared his throat. "I believe her," he said, and I shot him a grateful look. "I've seen what she's capable of. If any human can travel the ley, it makes sense that it would be the Fifth Crone."

"If she's really the Fifth," Percival muttered.

Protectors, I decided, were all pretty much jerks when you first met them.

Nia stepped into the conversation, directing their words to Maureen across the coffee table between the sofas. "Assuming her story is true," they began.

"Which we would be foolish to do," Yvain interrupted.

"Hush," Maureen told the protector. "Let your lady finish."

"It's not like we can just march in and set Elysabeth free," Nia said. "Morok himself must have placed the manacle on her —no Mage magick is strong enough. And, if that's the case, we don't stand a chance of breaking it. Unless ..."

They and Maureen turned their gazes on me, and my mug-holding hands stilled halfway to my mouth as I stared back at first one, then the other. At their expectations. *Shit*, I thought, seeking Lucan's gaze. I found it narrowed on me. Questioning. He knew something was up. He always knew.

And *later*, it seemed, had become now.

I lowered my tea to my lap and cleared my throat. "About that," I said.

The sound of splintering wood cut me off, and the room plunged into darkness but for the fire burning low in the grate.

CHAPTER 22

I SURGED TO MY FEET, BLANKET AND TEA FALLING TO THE floor, but I'd barely taken a step when Lucan shoved me down again and snarled, "Stay!" Then he just plain snarled, and I knew he'd morphed into wolf form.

Sudden flames flared high around Nia, blazed white hot, then gathered in their outstretched palm and shot outward toward a massive, serpentine shape winding through shattered shutters and onto the floor.

The snake creature reared back with a hissing screech—many hissing screeches—and my heart dropped to my toes as I got a good look at it. Multiple heads sprouted from its body—human heads. Each writhed independently. Each brushed the ceiling. Each had a mass of snakes sprouting from it in turn. And all the mouths—human and snake alike—had wide, curved mouths and pointed fangs that dripped goddess knew what kind of venom as their collective body coiled and uncoiled its way toward the Crones across from me.

Nia's fire missed it by inches and set the wall behind it ablaze. Unscathed, the giant snake-thing lunged forward, all its heads aiming for the Fire Crone.

The gargoyle threw itself into the path, blocking the attack and giving both the women time to retreat to a corner. It wrapped stone arms around the snake's body and squeezed, but the snake simply dragged it along as it slithered forward, seeming not to even notice.

By the light of the flames devouring floral wallpaper and centuries-old wood trim, I saw a black wolf—not Lucan's—leap up and seize the creature at the junction from where its heads sprouted. The snake writhed, whipping the wolf from side to side, its many heads biting at him with their many fangs, but the wolf clung on, just beyond their reach.

A second wolf—smaller, gray, and also not Lucan's—landed on the creature's back, and the snake hiss-screeched again, its convulsions growing wilder as the combined weight of the animals brought it low.

A loud clap of thunder sounded, and a streak of lightning flashed from storm clouds that had gathered in a corner of the ceiling to strike the snake's coiled body. The creature's screech turned agonized, and the pungent odor of roasted flesh filled the room. Another bolt from another corner struck its tail.

Still on the floor, I watched Lucan's wolf crouch low, circling as he searched for an opening to join the others and end the fight. More white flames rolled outward from the Crones' corner and engulfed one of the serpent's heads; a bolt of lightning struck another. Nia and Maureen's attack was coordinated. Controlled. Measured. The power of Fire and Air working together.

But as the storm clouds roiled, the accompanying wind roared through the room, fanning the flames, feeding them, spreading them. I hissed out a breath. That wasn't good. Coordinated and controlled as the attack might be, Anne's Water connection would also be useful—or mine, if I had any chance of accessing it.

Another set of shutters exploded into the room as a shade crashed through a window and joined the melee. A second one followed—this one coming straight at me.

I rolled away and scrambled to my feet. From the corner of my eye, I saw Lucan's wolf leap at the serpent, twist in midair to change direction, and aim for the shade hurtling toward me. Instinctively, I held out my hand, palm toward the creature as I had done when one had come through my bedroom window in my before-life.

But there was still only cold at my core, and no fire shot from my hand, controlled or otherwise. Shit.

Shit, shit, *shit.*

Lucan's body thudded into the shade's, and they rolled together across the floor, snarling and shrieking. Even if I could have brought myself to watch the battle, I had no time. Maureen and Nia were still focused on the snake their protectors fought, and the second shade was homing in on them.

I scrambled to my feet, grabbed the nearest thing at hand, and pitched it at the shade. A mug of tea exploded against the cruelly beaked head, and the creature flapped to a halt. Its yellow eyes fastened on me, and it changed direction, wings outstretched and black, barbed feathers glistening in the fire-light. Too late, I remembered Lucan's warning about how those feathers released from the shades and embedded in their victims to deliver their lethal toxin.

Did I mention *shit?*

Frantically, I scanned the room. *Weapon. I need a—*

My gaze landed on the tip of a stick sticking out from beneath the slipcovered sofa I'd been sitting on. My staff. I dived for it, my fingers closing around it as the shade hit my back and knocked me flat. The wind left my lungs in a grunt, and razor-sharp talons raked over my shoulders, seeking purchase, stopped only by the protective magick of the cloak I wore. I felt the fabric give way under the attack and knew the garment wouldn't hold up long under the talons scrabbling to pierce it. Biting back a scream and blinking away tears of pain, I tugged the linden staff from under the sofa.

If there had ever been an appropriate time for an inert stick to grow into a sentient tree again and protect me, now was it. But the staff lay unmoving in my grasp, and I had no choice but to go with Plan B. I gripped it in both hands, twisted it over my shoulder, and jabbed backwards with all my strength. The end of the staff sank into the shade's feathered body, surprising it enough that it released me and flapped backward—for about a millisecond.

It was long enough.

Forever grateful to Lucan for the self-defense lessons—and to past-me for keeping up the practice in his absence, however half-heartedly—I flipped onto my back, shifted my hold, and swung with all my strength as the shade came at me. The staff connected hard—harder than I'd thought myself capable of—and sent the creature cartwheeling through the air, straight at the snake.

Multiple, powerful jaws snapped shut, and fangs pierced feathers and bone alike—but not without consequence. Even as the serpent tried to shake the shade free, barbed feathers released, burying themselves in the snake's mouths, and all the heads screamed in agony as the toxins entered the shared body. The snake thrashed wildly, and the two wolves dangling from it released their holds and leaped clear, landing one on either side of the women who wielded fire and storm. The gargoyle squeezed harder. Grimly, through the violent spasms wracking the serpent's body and the flames devouring the walls and ceiling around it, the winged stone creature hung on, keeping the snake and its victim away from the others.

Then a resounding *crack* boomed through the room, and a huge, blazing beam dropped from the ceiling. It swallowed snake and stone alike in flames so hot, they scorched my face from across the room.

Behind me, Lucan's wolf yelped in pain. I spun on my heel and charged toward him, staff clutched like a baseball bat over my shoulder.

I EDGED AROUND THE TANGLE OF LUCAN AND SHADE, searching for an opening and a chance to swing. But between the smoke billowing through the room and my stinging, watering eyes, it was impossible to tell where wolf ended and monster began.

The entire room was ablaze. Snake flesh sizzled and stank.

Flames danced across the ceiling in sheets and ran down the walls in rivulets, throwing wild shadows everywhere. Some looked alive, and twice my heart jolted as I swung at one that came too close. Both times I connected with nothing, and I cursed my raw nerves for distracting me from helping my —Lucan.

Just Lucan, I reminded myself as I sidled left, right, then left again. Not *my* anything. Especially not since I'd found Elysabeth. I tamped down a little flare of something that felt remarkably like grief and focused on the combatants.

Wolf and shade remained locked together. I thought Lucan had it by the throat, but I couldn't be sure. Nor could I be sure his yelp hadn't been due to feathers embedding themselves in his flesh. Even if it hadn't, I didn't know how much longer he could last against the shade. I tightened my grip on my staff and did another quick search inside myself for anything remotely resembling magick, hoping against hope that a tiny part of it might have returned.

But there was nothing. I felt hollower than I had in my entire life, including during my marriage, and that was saying something.

A presence loomed at my back, and I had no time to dwell on my loss. I whirled, and my staff arced out from my shoulder. A strong hand caught it mid-swing, and Yvain's glittering blue eyes dared me to try again. Out of sheer frustration—not to mention the adrenaline rushing through my veins—I might well have done so, if Maureen hadn't stepped between us.

"Yvain!" she said, her sharp voice raised above the din of snarls and screams. "Help Lucan."

Yvain pushed my staff down and away from his Crone, his lip curled in a snarl. Maureen gave his shoulder a shove, and with a low, throaty rumble in his chest, he morphed into his wolf and sprang into the fray. A third wolf—Percival—shot past and did likewise, and the shade went down under the snarling pile. A bloodcurdling shriek erupted from it and was cut off. Just like that, the battle was over.

But the fire wasn't.

Rivulets of flame had become roaring, crackling rivers, flowing over the room. Devouring it. Seeking to devour us. Heat seared my skin and eyes. An ember dropped onto my shoulder and reflexively, I grabbed it and flung it away, memories of the fire pixies surging up in my mind. Except then, I'd had magick. Now—

Maureen caught hold of my hand and tugged, towing me after her toward the downed shade and the wolves standing over it. "The house has fallen, and more will be coming," she said. "We need to get out of here. Yvain!"

Now I had nothing.

Could *do* nothing.

The largest of the wolves morphed into human form again. Lucan and the other followed suit, and Nia joined us, a hastily gathered bundle of clothing clutched in their arms. The protectors took no time to dress, however. Instead, as the two women pulled me close, they formed a naked circle around us with their arms extended and hands locked onto one another's forearms. Chunks of burning wood rained down on them, and the acrid stench of singed hair filled my nostrils. I met Lucan's eyes across the tight circle.

"What—" I began, but I had no time to finish as the group stepped as one to the left, carrying me with it. Too late, I saw the faint shimmer of a ley line against the crackling flames.

Too late by far, I realized it was the wrong one.

CHAPTER 23

LEY TRAVEL WITH A MAGICKAL BEING WAS NOTHING LIKE travel on my own. There was no dissolution of body and mind. No soul-devouring agony. And I blessedly didn't puke my guts out on arrival.

Instead, it felt like the Earth dropped away from my feet, sending me into a freefall before an invisible something lifted me into the air and whirled me up and sideways and then down again, speeding up, slowing down, repeating. It wasn't unlike a roller coaster ride, but without the mechanical jarring and gut-wrenching terror. And when it ended, we just ... were.

Still standing. Still in our tight-knit bunch within the circle of naked arms. And in what looked to be the front entry of a house I didn't recognize, which meant we were still in the wrong place.

"No," I whispered. Shaking my head, I repeated, my voice rising with every word, "No, no, no. We went the wrong way. Damn it, Lucan, we have to go back!"

Lucan released his grip on his fellow protectors' wrists and came around to me. He put his hands on my shoulders.

"Milady, you saw the medusa and the shades. If we go back, the Mages will send something else—perhaps worse."

If by *medusa* he meant the many-human-headed snake, I didn't know what else *could* be worse. Other than the goliath, of course, which might not be technically worse but was certainly just as bad. I shuddered at the idea, and then shivered, and then quaked. *Reaction*, I thought. *It's just reaction.* But knowing what it was didn't stop it. My teeth clacked together so hard I was sure they'd shatter, and every muscle in my body tensed until I was rigid from head to toe. Strong arms went around me, holding me close.

Part of my brain noted that a naked Lucan was warm and solid and just the right kind of cuddly. Another part giggled with all the maturity of my inner twelve-year-old. I ferociously told both parts to shut up and pushed him away to arms' length, my hands—one still gripping the staff—planted against his chest.

"You don't understand," I said. "I can't take you to her from here. The ley she's on, the one I traveled to get to her, it's the one that runs through their house"—I pointed to Nia—"and ours. Elysabeth's. Whatever. The point is, we have to go back to it. It's the only way I—"

"Claire."

Lucan's voice cut across my own, and I stopped dead in astonishment. He'd used my name. Called me Claire. Not *Lady Claire* or even *milady*. Just Claire. I gaped at him as a ripple of surprise went through the group around us. He ignored it and focused on me.

"We can't go back," he said. "Mages will be waiting for us there. The ley we traveled to get here is at the other end of the house from where we found you. We'd never make it to yours. We'll have to take a different one to get back to the house, and then we can go to the Earth Crone from—"

"I think it's a trap," Nia murmured. "A funnel."

"Explain," Yvain said, his arms crossed over his chest. At some point during my spewing of words, he and Percival had managed to get dressed, and only Lucan remained naked—and distractingly near.

My twelve-year-old snickered again. I sent her to her room and slammed a mental door against her. I needed focus right now, not hysterical hormone-antics. And not this aching desire to return to Lucan's arms for their comfort, either.

I focused fiercely on Nia's words.

"If Lady Claire is right," they were saying, "and Elysabeth is on the ley line that runs through both the Earth and Air houses, then the Mages just destroyed our only direct route—the one that would have let us bypass Earth on our way to her."

"Which means we have no choice but to go to the Earth house first," Maureen said. "And you think that's what they want us to do?"

"You think they'll be waiting for us," Percival said. It was a statement rather than a question, but Nia answered it anyway.

"They obviously know where it is," Nia responded, "so yes. I do. I think they've systematically searched out and destroyed the other houses, so we'd have no choice but to gather there."

"Which means they'll come for us here, too," said Percival.

"As soon as they find us," the Fire Crone agreed.

Maureen was shaking her head. "But it doesn't make sense. How could they know Lady Claire would even find the ley line in the first place?"

The debate around me faded into the background as a bubble of horror slowly formed in my brain. Puzzle pieces began to fall into place. Kate's visit to the house. Her news that the Mages were gathering in Confluence. Twenty of them, at the four points of the compass—the four points representing the four elements. Twenty of them, in groups of five. Five being the number of ...

"But why would they not simply wait for us in Elysabeth's cell? Why go to all this trouble?" Maureen was asking. "What's so special about the Earth house?"

"Chaos," I whispered.

"Milady?" Lucan's bare chest rumbled beneath my hands, and I realized I still rested them against him. And that he was back to addressing me formally. I lowered my arms, one hand clenched in a fist to my side, the other holding onto the staff as if it were the only thing keeping me from being sucked into a maelstrom I might not be able to escape.

Because it was. And I might not.

"The Mages are gathering," I told Lucan. "In Confluence." I looked around the group, my explanation tumbling out in jarring bits and pieces. "That's where the house is. Confluence, Ontario. Anne called it a place of power that connects us to land, water, and sky. She's Indigenous—Anishinaabe, I think. I should have asked, but I didn't because Kate was there and we —" Babbling. I was babbling. I should stop that. I took a breath. "Because we had to decide what to do."

"Do about what?" Maureen asked.

"The Mages." The breath hadn't helped. The bubble of horror had continued to grow, pressing against the insides of my skull. I stared at the whitened knuckles of the fingers clenched around the wood. My knuckles but not mine, because I could see them but not feel them. "Kate said there were twenty of them, in groups of five at each of the four corners. Anne thinks they might be planning to tap into Confluence's power, and so ..."

From the corner of my eye, I saw Maureen and Nia look at one another, the same alarm in their expressions that had flared in Anne's eyes at Kate's news. They knew about the chaos, too.

"And so?" Lucan prompted.

"We brought my family to the house. For protection," I said. The bubble burst, and the horror it had contained—the utter, soul-destroying, all-consuming knowledge that this, all of this, was on me—flooded my entire being. I'd played right into the Mages' hands. I'd thought I was protecting my family by bringing them to the Earth house. Instead, I'd put them right in the center of things: Paul, Natalie, little Braden.

And now the remaining Crones were being funneled into that same center. Into that same place of power that was just as likely to work against them as for them.

Into chaos.

"Fuck," I croaked into the silence that followed my confession. I couldn't bring myself to look at any of our group, especially not Lucan, who would understand the full implication of my words. Lucan, who had already seen me take the pendant from around my neck once and offer it to the Mages in exchange for my family's safety. Lucan, who knew that it had only been Kate's actions—Kate dropping the pendant back into place around my neck and shoving me into a battle I hadn't wanted—that had prevented me from doing the unforgiveable.

He may have seen my strength, but he had also seen my weakness, and—

"Milady," a new voice interrupted. "Shall I bring tea?"

"Dear goddess!" I bellowed, rounding on the newcomer—a hapless gargoyle that was twice my size and looked like the devil himself carved in stone. "What is *with* your kind and bloody *tea*?"

Shock dropped over our company, and all eyes turned to me. Again. For someone who didn't particularly like being the center of attention, I was drawing an awful lot of it to myself lately. I groped with my second hand for my staff and curled my fingers around it above the first, desperately reaching for the protection of the linden from which it had come. Needing it to ground me. Center me.

To be more than just a stick.

It wasn't.

Because, on top of everything else, my fucking magick was gone.

My hands shook, and I sucked in a ragged breath. *Don't tell them about that,* I thought. *Not yet. Tell Lucan first. He'll know what to do.*

"I'm sorry," I told the open-mouthed gargoyle. "I really am. That was rude and uncalled for."

The gargoyle raised a thin eyebrow that was carved in its face —unlike Keven, it had actual ones—and shrugged. It swung its devil-horned head toward Maureen.

"Milady?" it prompted, as if I hadn't even spoken, let alone shrieked at it like some harridan.

"Yes," Maureen said, her gaze resting on me. "Yes, I think all our nerves could use some calming."

I STARTED SHAKING AGAIN WHEN THE GARGOYLE (BY process of elimination, I knew it to be Maureen's gargoyle) left the entry hall. I wondered how long it would take the Mages and their monsters to track us here to the Fire Crone's house—how long we would have before we had to pit our magick against theirs again in a war we appeared to be losing.

Well. Maureen and Nia would pit their magick against the Mages. I, on the other hand, would wave my non-magick stick and keep trying not to die a horrible death at the claws of a shade—or worse. My shivers increased, and I clamped my arms around myself.

Lucan had taken his clothes from Nia and begun dressing beside me. Nia murmured something to Maureen, whose gaze swept over me from head to foot and back again before she nodded in apparent agreement.

"Rest," she declared. "We all need it. I'll have the gargoyle bring the tea to your rooms, and we'll talk again at dinner."

But the Mages, my brain objected. *And Elysabeth and Paul and Natalie and Braden and—*

None of the objections made it off my tongue, however. It was too wooden—too exhausted—to form them. And if my tongue was too exhausted for words, I was pretty sure the rest of me was in equal need of the rest Maureen proposed.

"Are we safe enough?" I asked. Not safe, full-stop, because that state had ceased to exist. Just safe enough to rest. To gather our wits. To catch our breath.

"For a while. The Mages, like—" Maureen paused and regarded me, then shrugged and said, "Like the four elemental Crones, the Mages need magickal creatures to ferry them through the ley lines. We did enough damage at Nia's house that they'll need to find new ones. We should be fine for a day or two."

We should, but what about Elysabeth? But I could summon neither energy nor words for argument—or even agreement—and so I retreated into silence.

Maureen called the gargoyle back and, in short order, revised the tea request and made dinner arrangements. Then she led the way up the sweeping staircase—a marble one in this house—that led from the entry to the second-floor corridor. At the top, she pointed to the first door on the left as being her own and the one opposite as Percival's.

"Nia, the next two are for you and Yvain"—she pointed—"and Claire, yours and Lucan's are at the end of the hall. I'll have the gargoyle call you when dinner is ready."

I followed Lucan down the corridor, content to let him lead while I focused on keeping my legs from folding under me. There were pot lights in the ceiling here, rather than the wall sconces of the Earth house, and the floor was marble like the stairs, with a deep-red, Turkish-style carpet runner.

It was interesting how the houses differed from one another, I thought vaguely. The layouts seemed the same, from what I'd seen so far, but the interiors differed vastly from the stone and wood of my own ... of Elysabeth's ... of the Earth house. Perhaps one day, when life was normal again—or at least not utter chaos —I would have the chance to ask about that.

I heard the click of a door closing behind me, then another. But only two, and I put out a hand to the embossed paper on the wall so I wouldn't fall over as I risked a glance over my shoulder in time to see Yvain and Percival shift into wolf form outside their respective Crones' bedchambers. Each curled up on the carpet runner before the women's doors, and the pot lights above them dimmed. Each stared unblinkingly down the hall at me.

I turned away again and found Lucan waiting, his hand on the door handle of a room that was in the same place as mine in the Earth house. I pushed away from the wall and walked the last few steps to join him. He made no move to open the door.

"You shouldn't have come," he said. "You should have sent Bedivere."

I tried to raise an eyebrow at him, but it was about as functional as my tongue and barely twitched. If he thought I could convince his brother to do anything at all, let alone leave Anne, he hadn't been paying much attention back at the Earth house.

Lucan's mouth drew tight, and his voice was rough as he added, "You promised to stay safe."

Guilt twisted through me. "Things changed. I had no—" I stopped myself, remembering his words to me before he'd left the Earth house. Because he'd been right; I *had* had a choice. I'd had a lot of choices, and I'd made them all. Me. No one else. I could have told Kate *no* and sent my family back to their own home. I could have told Anne about the ley line when I first spotted it, before I stepped into it and found Elysabeth.

Just as I could have left before any of this had begun. Or ignored the address the pendant revealed in my newspaper on that very first morning. Or made any one of a dozen decisions other than the ones I had.

I could have turned away at any point, he'd said.

Could have but didn't.

And now, for better or for worse, the choices had been made. *My* choices had been made.

Including the one now, where I put my hand over his, twisted the doorknob, and then stepped into my room.

"Things changed," I said again, and then I closed the door, leaving him on the outside and—for now—taking the secret of my missing magick with me, because I was just too damned tired to share it. Even with him.

CHAPTER 24

A KNOCK AT MY DOOR WOKE ME WHEN THE LIGHT OUTSIDE the bedchamber window had dimmed to evening. I was both surprised and not to find that I'd slept. I didn't know how time worked with ley travel, but when I'd fallen onto the bed—fully clothed again, because that was how I seemed to roll these days —it felt like I'd gone a week without sleep.

But, then again, I didn't suppose that the effect of ley travel on time was the issue.

Its effect on me, however …

I rolled onto my side and curled around the cold at my core, hugging myself in an effort to restore warmth. I suspected the attempt was futile. Another knock sounded at the door.

"I'm awake," I called. "Thank you."

The door opened, and Lucan stood framed against the light in the corridor behind him, holding something in an outstretched hand. "Lady Nia thought you might like clean clothes."

I looked down at myself. The cloak wrapped around me was again clean and unscathed because of the magick woven into it, but the pants and shirt beneath hadn't fared quite so well. Both were streaked with soot and ash, I'd lost three buttons from the shirt, and a long tear in one pantleg exposed my knee and most of my thigh. I hadn't even noticed.

My nose wrinkled as I registered the acrid stench of smoke clinging to me. It wasn't as awful as the smell that had followed me from Elysabeth's cell, but nonetheless, I—or at least, my clothes—stank. I hadn't noticed that, either.

"Yes," I said. "That would be nice."

He came into the room and set a pile of clothes on the foot of the bed. I hoped against hope that Nia had thought to include clean underwear among them. And that I had time for a shower before dinner, because—I sniffed the hair lying beneath my cheek—nope, it wasn't just my clothes that stank.

"Lady Claire."

Lucan's voice carried a *we need to talk* tone, and I closed my eyes for a moment. While I'd managed to avoid the conversation earlier by shutting the door on him, I couldn't do so forever, and we did need to talk. More precisely, *I* needed to.

I swung my legs over the side of the bed and sat up, pulling the cloak around me with one hand, then poking the other out from under it to push back my hair. Then, because there was no point in beating about the bush, I took a deep breath and blurted, "I've lost my magick."

Amber eyes stared at me. Clearly, that was not the news Lucan had expected.

"Duh," said my Claire-voice. Why couldn't that have been the voice I'd lost touch with, instead of Edie's?

"I beg your pardon?"

"In the ley lines, I think." I curled my fingers into the duvet cover beneath me, pushing away the ache of loss that had replaced my warmth. I needed to deal with this first—my confession ... my truth ... whatever the hell it was. Which meant full disclosure.

"It's gotten weaker each time I've traveled," I said. "At first, I thought something in Elysabeth's cell was responsible—some kind of trap laid by Morok, because I was still able to call Fire there. Enough to make and hold light, anyway, and the staff—" I untangled my fingers to point at the linden rod leaning against a wardrobe that was an exact match to mine at the Earth house. "The staff sent a shoot into the wall and cracked it to bring water for her. But when I returned to the Earth house, recovery was harder, and I couldn't find the Fire connection at all."

"And the other connections?"

"I didn't think to try them. Lessons with Anne weren't as helpful as we hoped, and I couldn't—I wasn't—" I broke off, not wanting to admit that I had made no progress in his absence. That I had failed him. Then I raised my chin. *Full disclosure.*

"I didn't have time to play around with something I couldn't do in the first place," I said. "Then, after the last trip—the one to find you and the others—well, you saw for yourself what it did to me. I could hardly stand up on my own, let alone straight, and ..."

Lucan's face had taken on a grim set. "And what?"

"And when the snake thing—the medusa—and the shades attacked, I had nothing." I shrugged with a nonchalance that, in truth, I was light years from feeling, because what I really wanted to do was throw myself into his arms and beg him to hold me. Ached to hear him tell me everything would be all right. But that wasn't going to happen, was it? Because he knew about Elysabeth now, and his responsibility was to her, not me.

So was my responsibility, because I'd made a promise.

"I'm cold inside," I said, "where I used to find Fire. And the linden staff"—the staff-slash-wand Lucan himself had carved for me—"doesn't respond to me anymore. It doesn't ... fit." I curled my empty hand into a fist beneath my cloak. "My magick is gone, Lucan."

And nothing would ever be right again.

"WELL," SAID MAUREEN WHEN I FINISHED REPEATING MY tale to the group. She looked over at Nia, who sat next to me, and then around the table at the shifters: Lucan, silent beside me; Percival at the opposite end from her; Yvain beside Nia.

I stared down at the untouched plate of food before me, not needing to follow her gaze to see the shock on the others' faces. Not when it sat so thick and still over the room. So silent.

"Well," she said again.

Nia cleared their throat. "You're sure?" they said. "You might just be tired. You've had a rough few days, traveling the ley by yourself the way you did, and—"

"I'm sure." I lifted my head to meet their dark eyes. Their stunned-by-my-revelation eyes. "I think the ley travel might still be to blame, but, yes, I'm sure it's gone."

"If it was ever there to begin with," muttered Yvain beside them.

Lucan glowered at him and opened his mouth to respond. I put my hand on the forearm he rested beside his plate. His teeth snapped shut with an audible clack. I withdrew my hand and met Yvain's hard stare across the table.

"Whether you believe me or not isn't the point," I said wearily. "The point is, I'm of no help now"—no magickal help, anyway, because yee haw, I could still knock a shade into the jaws of a medusa through sheer physical force, damn it—"and we still need to find a way to rescue Elysabeth."

The shifter's expression turned sour, but after a sidelong look at his Crone—who, I suspected, had just kicked him under the table—he subsided into tight-lipped silence. Or sulking.

With shifters, there didn't seem to be much difference.

"More tea?" rumbled a voice behind me.

I looked over my shoulder and summoned what little smile I could for the devil gargoyle that served the Air house. "No," I said, glancing at my still-full cup. "Thank you, but I'm fine."

"Huh," it grunted, then pointed to the roasted venison and root vegetables, long since cold. "And that?"

Keven always took it as a personal affront when I didn't eat what she'd prepared—a comment on her cooking. Would this gargoyle do the same? I tried harder for the smile, but I was pretty sure it turned into a grimace of apology. "I'm sorry, I'm just not very hungry. But it was delicious."

The stony gaze moved to my clean, unused fork, but the gargoyle made no comment as it collected utensils and plate alike, then traveled around the table, picking up similarly untouched meals from my dinner companions. Even perpetually hungry Lucan had left most of his.

We were in rough shape.

The gargoyle departed again, carrying the tray of dishes. The door swung shut behind it, and at the head of the table, Maureen cleared her throat.

"I propose we break until morning," she said. "Maybe a good night's sleep—"

"I disagree," Lucan said. "Nothing will have changed in the morning, and the longer we wait, the longer the Mages have to prepare for our arrival at the Earth house. I say we go for the element of surprise."

"As in *surprise, she has no magick*?" Yvain growled, pointing at me. "I'm sure they'd shake in their boots."

Like the dining room table at the Earth house, the one here was round; unlike the chairs at the Earth house, however, these ones had arms. It was a nice touch. I particularly liked how it gave Lucan something to hold onto, so he didn't lunge across the table at the other shifter, as I suspected he wanted to do. I debated putting out a hand to him again but opted not to, preferring not to lose it.

On my left, Percival cleared his throat, and then, to my surprise—and Yvain's disgust, judging by the other's eyeroll—he backed up Lucan.

"Surprise might be good," he murmured. He sat back in his chair, resting an elbow on the arm of his chair, with a thumb hooked under his clean-shaven chin and a forefinger across his mouth. "What do you have in mind?"

"Seriously?" Yvain demanded. "You really want to stick our collective heads in Morok's noose based on what this—"

"Careful, Yvain," Nia interrupted. "You're talking about a Crone."

"I'm talking about someone who admits she has no power and has helped Morok set his trap," the shifter retorted. "That is no Crone, milady, and we have no idea what her agenda might—"

"Oh, for fuck's sake!" I slammed both hands on the table—carefully, this time, because I remembered all too well the sting of my palms the last time I'd tried to get everyone's attention this way.

I thrust myself to my feet and leaned across the table, meeting Yvain's hostility glare for glare. "First Bedivere, and now you. What the hell do I have to do to prove I'm not aiding and abetting goddamn Morok? Do you really think I helped him on *purpose*? My family is back at that house, Yvain —my *grandson*. Why, in the name of every god and goddess who ever existed, would I put a *child* in the path of the Mages and their monsters?"

A hand settled over one of mine on the table. "Milady," Lucan murmured.

I shook him off as fury boiled over inside me—cold fury, because I still had no heat at my core, for which Yvain should thank his lucky stars at the moment.

"No," I said. "No, damn it. I am sick to death of being dismissed, Lucan. By them, by Keven—even by you." I returned my glare to Yvain. "I traveled the ley lines four times—*four*—without anyone there to protect me, and each time I was taken apart and reassembled and fucking *scrambled*, so is it any wonder my magick is gone?"

"But make no mistake, protector," I continued, neither expecting nor waiting for Yvain's response, "because this?" I leaned closer and tugged my pendant from inside my shirt. *My* pendant. I held it out, dangling it from the fist in which I clenched its chain. It twirled, glinting as it caught the light. "*This* is still the pendant of a Crone, damn it. The Fifth Crone. I didn't ask for it, I didn't want it, and I sure as fuck didn't need to have my entire life turned upside down by it, but here it is anyway."

Letting the pendant drop back onto my chest, I straightened to my full height and lifted my chin to stare down at the silent

shifter across from me as I went in for the close on the best—
and probably only—rant in my life. "So, yes," I said proudly,
"Yes, Yvain, I *am* Cro—"

A thunderous roar swallowed the rest of my declaration, and
the dining room ceiling collapsed onto the table.

CHAPTER 25

MY FIRST THOUGHT AS I BOUNCED OFF THE WALL, courtesy of a shove from Lucan, was that I was getting damned tired of being pushed out of the way. Then, as a familiar and unwelcome shriek shredded my eardrums, I quickly revised that feeling of annoyance to one of gratitude.

So much gratitude.

Because shades. Plural. The collapse of the ceiling had taken out the chandelier, and plunged the room into darkness, but Nia's fire flared in the far corner within seconds and illuminated —dear goddess—a veritable stream of the foul, black-winged creatures pouring in through the ragged hole above us. They tangled with one another atop the ruined table, screeching and fighting amongst themselves as they mindlessly sought their prey.

As they sought us.

Chaos unfolded as I pressed myself into the corner where Lucan had thrown me. Nia and Maureen stood shoulder to shoulder, their backs to the wall opposite me. White flames shot from Maureen's palms and ragged lightning from thick black clouds conjured by Nia, but the roiling mass of shades—six of them—avoided bolt after flame after bolt. To either side of the two women crouched their snarling protectors, ready to fight to the death for their Crones—a death that would be unavoidable if we stayed in this room with the creatures. With so many of them milling about in an enclosed space like this, avoiding their barbed feathers would be impossible.

Especially for me, because there was no sign of Lucan in the melee, and without my connection to magick—controlled or otherwise—I was helpless. Useless. And decidedly nothing like the Crone I'd just proclaimed myself to be.

181

I tried to find it. Goddess knows, I tried. As slitted yellow eyes turned in my direction and one of the shades unraveled itself from the others, I almost ruptured something, I tried so hard to find a connection. Any connection: Fire, Earth, Air, Water ...

But my efforts were in vain. My core remained cold, I remained hollow, and the shade's talons reached for my head as it flapped toward me. And I didn't even have my staff to protect me. Death, it seemed, was imminent.

In that weird phenomenon I'd heard about but never before experienced, my world slowed. Micro-fragments of the life I'd lived flashed through my mind. Memories. Images. The choices I'd made.

I thought about how I'd once feared dying alone and feeble in my house. About the purpose I had found in a pendant, a house, a gargoyle, a shifter. I thought about the family I'd left behind. The rocky terms on which Paul and I had parted. Elysabeth, who would die waiting for—

A hand seized my arm in a grip like iron and yanked me to the side as the shade's talons grazed my head, so close they raked through my hair—but not my skin. I opened eyes I hadn't even known I'd closed and found Lucan, still in human form, towing me toward the open dining room door. He yelled at the others about a ley line in the kitchen. Ordered them, through the cacophony of the shades' screeches, to follow.

From the corner of my eye as I stumbled in his wake, I saw Yvain and Percival shift into human form again and push their Crones toward us, and then we were through the door and into the hall, and the devil gargoyle was charging past us into the melee, and—

Lucan shoved something into my hand as he thrust me through another doorway. I barely had time to blink in recognition of my staff before Maureen and Nia crowded against me and the protectors' arms encircled us, hands clamped over one another's wrists.

"Wait!" I pulled Lucan's hand away from its grip on Percival's arm. "Where are we going?"

"Earth house," Lucan said.

"But we have no plan. We need—" I broke off, because I didn't know how to finish. We needed many things. We needed more of us and fewer of our Mage enemies. We needed me to have my power back.

We needed a fucking miracle.

I flinched from a howl of agony coming from the dining room, followed by a guttural roar of triumph like a rockslide down a mountain. One shade down, five to go—if the gargoyle could hold out against them. If not—the still-open kitchen door loomed beyond our circle.

"We cannot wait," Percival growled.

I looked at the faces surrounding me—the understanding in them that we would have none of the things we needed. Their determination to forge on, regardless. I gritted my teeth. We weren't leaving without a plan, damn it.

I released Lucan's arm and ducked out of the protectors' circle, dodging Maureen's attempt to hold me back. I slammed the kitchen door shut and cast about for something to hold it. Percival broke rank first. He strode to the massive harvest table, identical to the one I'd sat at so many times at the Earth house and, with a grunt, flipped it on its side. Wordlessly, Yvain and Lucan joined him, and together they pushed the table against the door. Percival turned to me.

"That gains us roughly thirty seconds. Talk fast."

I whirled to Lucan. "Where will this ley come out at the Earth house?"

"I don't know."

Shit. I tried to think faster. The panic trying to claw its way out of my chest was not my brain's friend.

"Twenty-seven seconds," said Percival.

Fuck.

"Fine. Wherever it comes out and whatever we find, we

separate the second we get there," I said. "Maureen and Nia, you find Anne and stay with her. Lucan and I will get Elysabeth."

The objections were immediate.

"What if she's too weak to be moved?" Maureen asked.

"You'll need magic to break the manacle," said Nia.

And my favorite—from Yvain, of course. "Why *you*?"

I addressed them one at a time. "If she can't stand, we'll carry her; and if Lucan can't break the manacle, then we'll carry the damned bed, too. And why me?" I looked Yvain square in the face. "Because A, I know where Elysabeth is in the ley, and B, we cannot, under any circumstances, let the Earth house fall to the Mages. It's all we have left."

The protector didn't back down. "She is Lucan's Crone. Surely he could sense her presence in the ley."

"And if he can't?"

Yvain's mouth went tight. Percival cleared his throat.

"Beg pardon, milady, but there's no guarantee you can, either. Not without your magick."

A tiny silence fell, because he was right. We were all right. Something hit the other side of the kitchen door. The table scraped several inches across the flagstone, and the door splintered. It wouldn't hold. We had to go. I went back to Maureen and Nia and wrapped my arms around them, staff gripped hard to make sure I didn't lose it—and to keep my hand from trembling. I looked at each of them, these women on whose shoulders the world rested.

"I'll bring her back," I promised as the protectors' arms encircled us again. Then, as the protectors stepped as one toward the ley that opened by the stove, I looked up at Lucan. "The line we need is in the garden. If we get separated, I'll meet you at the—"

The ley swallowed us.

CHAPTER 26

WE LANDED IN THE MIDDLE OF MAGES.

There were five of them, treading a circle they'd burned into the grass clearing on the north side of the Earth house. Hands joined and faces shadowed by hooded robes, they moved counterclockwise, their voices raised in a chant. And as surprised as we might have been to find ourselves there, the Mages were more so.

I didn't know what they'd been trying to conjure, but it wasn't two Crones and three protectors—and they didn't stand a chance. Lucan, Percival, and Yvain all morphed before I had even disentangled myself from Maureen and Nia, and by the time I dropped into a fighting stance, staff at the ready, all five of our enemies lay on the ground, their throats ripped out and their lives seeping into the earth.

They didn't even have time to cry out.

An enormous fireball roared through the sky and exploded over the roof of the house. Nia swiftly extinguished it with a wide sweep of her arm and a gust of wind. Cedar shakes rained down in its aftermath. We needed to move fast.

"Percival! With me," Maureen snapped, and the smallest of the wolves—still huge by most standards—fell in beside her. "I'll take the front," she told Nia as a scream erupted from that direction, "and you try to get inside. Claire—"

But I was staring in the direction the scream had come from. Fighting to breathe. Struggling not to fold into a heap on the grass. Because I knew that voice. I knew—

"Mommy!" cried a child's voice. "Mommy, get up!"

Braden.

Natalie.

Maureen grabbed at my arm, but I shook her off and bolted

toward the front of the house. Lucan's wolf joined me as I rounded the corner, trying to block my path. Blindly, I swung at him with the staff, my gaze fixed on the huddled group ahead of me. Lucan growled but gave way and ran beside me, and as we reached the figures, he changed back to his human form and dropped down on one bare knee beside them. Kate Abraham ran toward us from the house.

For a moment, I stood paralyzed, staring down at the tableau before me in disbelief. Horror. An agony worse than that inflicted by the ley line.

My son sat on the dirt path that bisected the front clearing, his wife's head and shoulders cradled in his lap. Tears tracked through the dust caked on his face, dripping from his chin onto Natalie's pale forehead. Her eyes were closed, her face still. Braden lay across her, his tiny arms wrapped around her waist, and his "Mamamamamama" an unbroken howl that laid open my heart. I put a hand over my mouth to hold back my answering wail.

"I'm so sorry," Kate panted as she reached us, her expression stricken. "They got away on me. He took Braden, and Natalie followed them, and—I'm so sorry." She dropped to her knees and put her fingers to Natalie's throat.

"Oh, Paul," I whispered behind my hand. "Why—"

My son looked up at me through his tears, and his face twisted, became ugly. "You did this," he hissed. "Not me. *You.*"

I flinched from the words. From the hatred that filled his eyes. I, too, dropped to my knees at his side, reaching for his shoulder. He knocked it away with so much force that I gasped, and my fingers went numb. "Paul—"

"She's alive," said Kate. "But we need to get her back to the house and away from this."

She nodded at the clearing, and I realized with a start that we knelt on a tiny island in the middle of a war zone awash with muddy water. It swirled into rivers and lakes, receded and swelled, like an ever-changing moat between house and woods—

between house and the red-hatted creatures trying to advance on it. As I watched, a wave surged up from the grass and smashed one against the trees. Shards of blue ceramic coat showered down into the seething waters below like bits of flotsam.

The garden gnomes had returned.

The memory of teeth sank into my hamstring, and I shuddered. I'd been so focused on my family, on Braden's grief, that I hadn't even seen them. But I did now. I saw it all: the surging water; the gnomes; Anne, who knelt in the doorway of the house, her sling abandoned and both hands flat on the flagstone porch as she called the water to her from the earth itself and sent it out again, her face taut with concentration.

I saw, absorbed, and remembered what needed to be done. What *I* needed to do.

Even if I didn't have my magick, even if I couldn't act as the Fifth Crone, the others—including Elysabeth—still needed to come together if we were to stand a chance of defeating Morok. They needed to split the world again, and—

I squeezed my eyes shut, remembering the conversation at the kitchen table with Keven and Lucan, when I had first learned about Morok-Merlin and how the Crones had kept him from destroying the world by trapping bits of his powers in the parts of the world they splintered off. How the 'cure' would ultimately be as devastating as the disease, because each division had weakened the world, and goddess knew how many splinters away from total destruction we were.

We could but pray that this next one wouldn't be it, because right now, it was our only chance—and I needed to do everything in my power to make it happen.

Thunder boomed in the sky behind the house, followed by the ear-splitting crack of a lightning bolt and the shriek of a dying shade. I opened my eyes and levered myself to my feet, staff held fast. "Kate is right," I told Paul. "We need to move her."

If not for Natalie's sake, then for Anne's, so she wouldn't

have so far to reach. So she could conserve her energy and—

"Touch her and I will rip your heart out," Paul snarled up at me.

Kate scowled and looked as though she might intervene, but a distant, guttural roar cut her off, and we both turned toward the woods. I'd heard that sound only one other time, but I could never forget it.

The Mages had summoned their goliath.

Kate's gaze met mine, and I nodded. I'd run out of time for wheedling and cajoling.

I bent at the waist and grasped my son's chin in my fingers, holding fast when he tried to twist away. "Enough," I said. "Hate me all you want, Paul, but later. Right now, I need you to do as you're told. Take your son into the house. Lucan will carry Natalie."

"Milady," Lucan began.

"Just do it, Lucan." I released my hold on my son and gently pulled my grandson away from his mother's belly. Crouched down on one knee, I wrapped my arms around him, pressing my lips against the side of his head. The goliath roared again. Was it closer? I couldn't tell. I shuddered. How long before it got here?

"Braden, listen to Grandma," I whispered. "Mommy is hurt, and we need to move her into the house, okay? I need you to be brave and help your dad. Can you do that for me?"

Sobs wracked the small frame resting against my chest, and Braden pulled back to look at me, his face wet with tears. "How bad is she hurt? Will she be dead?"

I wondered how many times my heart could shatter before it simply wouldn't function anymore. How much trauma one small child could endure before *he* wouldn't function.

But I had greater worries than that right now.

I injected all the calm and confidence I wished I could feel into my voice as I used the bottom of my cloak to wipe away tears and snot alike. "Your daddy is going to look after her," I assured him. "Isn't that right, Paul?"

My son glared at me but didn't disagree, and I turned my attention back to the child in my arms. "I'll be back as soon as I—"

"No, Grandma!" Braden threw his arms around my neck. "No! Don't go!"

Fuck.

"Milady, we have to move," Lucan murmured. He nodded toward the woods, and I saw that the gnomes had organized into a phalanx in the trees and begun a slow march toward the clearing, the underbrush falling before them. The air vibrated with the drumming of hundreds of footsteps, and Anne's waves were weakening. The goliath roared a third time.

Fuckity fuck, fuck, fuck.

"I have to go, sweetheart." I pried Braden's arms loose, my heart shredding in my chest. "But I promise I'll be back as soon as I can. Now go with Daddy, all right? I love you, Braden." I pushed my grandson—along with a giant chunk of my own soul —toward his father as Lucan lifted Natalie and Kate pulled Paul to his feet. "And I love y—"

You, too, I'd been about to say to my son, but his snarl cut me off. "You," he said savagely, scooping Braden into his arms, "will never see him again. Not ever."

I watched him stalk toward the house with his screaming child held fast against his shoulder—my stubborn, unyielding, *stupid* son—and knew he would do everything in his power to keep his word. Knew I had lost him, and with him, the last of my family. Knew, but didn't have the luxury of grief.

"Milady, the garden," Lucan urged.

"Yes," I said. "I'm going."

"I'll make sure she gets there," Kate said. Lucan nodded acceptance of the offer and, with Natalie hanging limp in his arms, strode off in Paul's wake. Kate fell into step beside me, sleeves rolled up, a long, gnarled wand extended at the ready in her right hand, and her left hand on my elbow, urging me forward.

"Where are the other midwitches??" I asked, breaking into an obedient trot. "How long can they hold out?"

"Most of them are inside. We came when we realized the Mages were focusing their attack here." She jerked her head toward the house, not breaking stride. "We were doing well until you got here—the Mages only had the gnomes and a couple of shades. Now ... well. At least we have the other Crones here to help."

"Or not," I said. As she helped me over the fence, I told her about the funnel trap theory Nia had put forward. "If she's right, they'll come at us with everything they have as soon as we bring Elysabeth back. I think they're holding the goliath back until then."

"Should you be bringing her back here, then?"

"Probably not." I scanned the garden, looking for the telltale glimmer of the ley line, hoping I would still be able to see it without my magick. "But we don't have much choice. All four Crones have to be together if they're going to stop Morok. I just hope ..."

"What?"

I tightened my fist around my staff and flashed a glance at her. "I'm not sure Elysabeth will be of any use when she gets here. Not in the condition she was in when I left her."

There. I saw the pale ribbon at last and started toward it.

"I can help with that," Kate said. She tugged a muslin bag from her pocket. "It should give her a healing boost. It needs a few minutes to take effect, but by the time she gets back here, she should be able to function—at least for a little while."

And there was Lucan, dressed again and coming out from the kitchen. I sagged a little in relief, in part at seeing him, in part at knowing Natalie was as safe as she could be for the moment.

As if he'd read my mind—because he probably had—his first words to me were, "I left her with Keven. She'll do all she can for her."

"Thank you."

He nodded. "Are you ready?"

"Yes." I reached for the bag of herbs Kate held, but she pulled it back.

"I'm not sure ..."

I frowned. "Not sure about what?"

She hesitated. "I don't want to insult you, but the herbs on their own aren't going to be enough. You need magick to activate them, and ..."

Fuckity-fuck.

"Then you'll have to come with us," I said. I turned to Lucan. "You can manage two of us, right?"

"I can, but getting three of you back could be challenging."

"Trust me, Elysabeth is so thin, you won't even have to stretch," I said grimly. Not caring what I trampled on, I led the way through the carrots to the shimmering ley line, then faced my companions. "Right. Let's do this," I said. "Let's bring her back."

I reached out and hugged Kate close. She wrapped her own arms around me in return, her cheek surprisingly cold against mine. Then Lucan stretched his arms around both of us and locked his fingers together. As the three of us stepped sideways as one, I let myself lean back, just a little.

On purpose or not, Lucan stood behind me, rather than Kate, and it was I who rested against his familiar chest for the journey. I who felt his strength. His warmth.

One last time, I thought. One precious, inestimable last—

Beyond Kate's shoulder, the trees suddenly turned black as crows poured from them. Hundreds of them rushed toward us, the flapping of their wings like the roar of a river, and I ducked as they passed overhead. Now what? I stumbled and tried to stop our little group's sideways step, but I was too late.

The icy magick of the ley closed over us, and the roller coaster swept us away.

CHAPTER 27

THE CROWS FOLLOWED US TO THE CELL.

Well. Me. They followed me to the cell, because even as I felt the tug of Elysabeth, and Lucan sensed whatever signal I unconsciously gave him, and we stepped out of the ley line, he and Kate remained oblivious to the rush of wings circling overhead.

They'd never come this close before—or been this persistent.

I ducked away from the brush of feathers against my face as the safe circle of Lucan's arms fell away. But in the dark—I'd forgotten how absolute it was—my brain couldn't decide which way was up, and I would have toppled if Kate hadn't tightened the hold she still had on my waist.

"Whoa there—you okay?"

I nodded, then remembered she couldn't see me. "I'm fine," I croaked, resisting the urge to flail at the wings beating overhead. I held myself rigid against the noise of the harbingers only I could hear—and against the rising unease in my chest. What were they trying to tell me?

I freed myself from Kate's hold, using my staff to keep my balance, so that I didn't flail at her, either. The crows in the cell with us flapped faster. Something was very, very wrong.

"You're sure this is it? I can see nothing," Lucan growled, his voice moving away to my left, "but I think I smell—"

"Be careful where you step!" I warned, but I was too late. Through the rushing river of wings, I heard the thunk of boot against metal, followed by his curse and a wet slosh as Elysabeth's waste bucket and its contents tipped over. I slapped a hand over my mouth and nose, but the fresh onslaught of putridness reached between my fingers anyway. I gagged. Kate did, too.

"Dear god," she muttered. "Was that what I think it was?"

"Mm." I replied, not wanting to open my mouth for actual words.

But I needed air.

I dropped my hand and resorted to mouth breathing, which helped. A little. Maybe.

"Light," I croaked, my voice made nasal by keeping my sinuses closed off in the back of my throat. "We need light."

"You can't—?" Kate broke off. "Never mind. I brought something in case."

A powerful beam of light sliced through the cell.

"A flashlight?" I stared at the beam's source in her hand. It looked like the police-issue one from her uniform.

"Anne told me about Elysabeth's manacle stopping her magick, and I wasn't sure if its dampening effect might extend to others," she said. "It seemed a good idea to play it safe."

She played the beam along the walls and over the mass of crows milling about in front of them, stopping at Lucan and dropping the light to the floor where he stood amid the thick, clotted sewage he'd knocked over.

"Sweet Jesus," Kate muttered. "This place ..."

My gorge rose. Yes. This place. And Elysabeth was still in it. Ignoring the prickles along my skin and the crow that flew straight at me, I pushed aside my unease and focused on our purpose here. The crow passed overhead, its wings brushing my scalp.

"She should be over that way." I extended a hand into the flashlight beam so Kate could see the finger I pointed toward the wall opposite Lucan. "On a cot."

Kate moved the flashlight, and the beam came to rest on what looked like a bundle of rags on an otherwise empty mattress. "There's no one—"

"That's her," I said. "That's Elysabeth."

The rags didn't move, but Kate and Lucan both did. She beat him to Elysabeth by a fraction of an instant and handed the flashlight to him. "Hold this," she ordered. "Let me check her."

I stayed where I was, holding my breath. The seconds slipped past. So did the crows—repeatedly—as they flapped in circles. My apprehensiveness returned tenfold, bringing with it a sense of urgency that all but made me dance on the spot. Whatever my harbingers were trying to tell me, we needed to get out of here.

"She's breathing," Kate said. "But only just, and she's not conscious, so there's no way I can get that potion into her. We need to get her back to the house. Keven will know better than me what to do."

I hunched against the feathered onslaught and joined her and Lucan at Elysabeth's bedside. My breath caught as I took in the wretched figure on the bed. The few days that had passed since I'd been here had taken a greater toll than I'd imagined possible. A crow dropped down from the murder above and huddled beside the Earth Crone's head, staring at me with a beady black eye.

"We can't possibly move her like this," I objected—and, dear goddess, what was with these damned crows?

"We have no choice."

"What about the manacle?" Lucan asked. "Can we break it?"

Kate picked up Elysabeth's wrist. "Definitely magick," she murmured, running her fingers over it. "And I don't think it will break under force, either. There's only one way ..." She spat into her hand a few times, then rubbed her saliva over the thin, paper-dry skin of Elysabeth's hand. Gently, she squeezed the bones together as she wriggled the metal bracelet, working it down over the Crone's hand until—slowly, grudgingly—it slipped off. We breathed a collective sigh of relief.

Then, before Lucan could do so, she stood and slid one arm beneath Elysabeth's knees and the other under her shoulders, straightening again without effort. She turned with her burden, the Earth Crone's arms and head hanging lifelessly. On the bed, the crow opened its beak but made no sound.

My unease became agitation, the crows above flew faster, and the cell walls felt like they were closing in on me. I didn't know what was wrong, or what was coming, but Kate was right. We needed to get out of here. I took the flashlight from Lucan with my free hand, my cold fingers brushing against his.

"You take Elysabeth, and I'll light the way back to the ley," I said, fighting the urge to let my touch linger on his warmth—and not just because it was him, because Goddess, I was missing my inner heat. I directed the beam toward floor. "This way."

I started toward the shimmer on the other side of the cell, but I'd barely taken three steps when Kate said, "Wait. This isn't going to work."

I shined the flashlight beam in her direction, keeping it out of her eyes. Lucan had moved toward her, his arms outstretched for Elysabeth, but Kate hadn't given her over. Above them, the crows no longer circled but flew erratically, their agitation reflecting—or perhaps feeding—my own as they collided with one another in mid-air. Black feathers rained down on the Crone in Kate's arms.

What? I wanted to scream at them. *What is coming? What are you trying to tell me?*

But Lucan forestalled me with his own question. "What won't work?" he asked Kate.

"You can't possibly take all three of us—not if we have to carry Elysabeth."

"We can hold her upright," I said. "Between us. Now come *on.*"

Kate handed Elysabeth's limp frame over to Lucan, and at last we were all moving in the right direction. The ley beckoned. The crows' erratic circles became more frenzied. By the time we stood together by the shimmering ribbon, my every nerve was stretched to breaking.

I pointed the light at the ceiling, and by its dull, ambient glow, Lucan eased Elysabeth to her feet, supporting her there as Kate and I moved to sandwich her between us. But as we closed our arms around the Earth Crone, she moaned—a low, keening cry of pain—and in an instant, Lucan's snarling wolf stood atop his abandoned clothing, ready to spring at our throats.

"Jesus fuck," Kate swore. She leapt away, leaving me to hold up the sagging Elysabeth alone—and to hope to hell that whatever small connection Lucan and I had would be enough to save me.

"Don't move," I whispered to Kate. "He's just trying to protect Elysabeth." I didn't look at her, didn't dare turn my head away from the wolf. My voice quavering, I said, "Lucan, it's me. It's Claire. I'm trying to help Elysabeth, remember? Not hurt her. Look. I'm putting her down now, all right? I'm putting her on the floor."

With the utmost gentleness, I lowered the frail, limp Earth Crone to the stone, trying to keep her out of the worst of the filth. Trying not to break her. Then, still crouching, I lifted my hands away from her and looked at Lucan again, holding the flashlight so I could see him.

For a moment, I saw nothing in his eyes but the animal the magick had made him into, then a faint recognition flickered in the amber depths. As fast as he had morphed into his wolf, Lucan returned to human form.

"Claire," he said hoarsely. "I'm—"

"Don't," I said. "I know that wasn't you." I eased myself upright and gestured with the flashlight beam at the form by my feet. "But it poses a problem, doesn't it?"

"It does." Lucan agreed grimly. His mouth tight, he tugged on his pants and picked up his shirt.

"Uh ..." said Kate. "Can we define problem?"

The crows' haphazard circles in the air above her continued. I'd forgotten them for a moment. And I was getting damned tired of their unsettling, unexplained presence.

"My change to wolf form isn't always by choice," Lucan said. He pulled the shirt over his heads and slid his arms into the sleeves. "Any perception of a threat triggers it."

"The sound Elysabeth made," Kate said. It was a statement

rather than a question, and Lucan didn't answer. He didn't have to.

He stooped to put his boots on, then straightened again and looked at me, raking the fingers of one hand through his long tangle of hair, pushing it back from his face. "If it happens in the ley ..." he said.

I didn't need him to finish. I'd already figured out the consequences for myself. And the only solution.

"We'll have to travel separately," I said decisively, ignoring the fact that I wanted to throw up at the very idea of more ley travel without the protection of a magickal being. "You take Elysabeth on your own."

"I can't leave you and Kate."

"And we can't—" I broke off, unwilling to say the words *trust you* to him, although that was what it amounted to. I settled for, "Kate and I will follow."

"We don't even know that you can, without your—" It was his turn to stop mid-sentence. He shot a look at Kate.

She frowned, glancing between us. "Without what?"

"My magick," I said, because she had the right to know. "I've lost it."

"Lost—" She gaped at me. "All of it? You're sure?"

I flapped a hand at a crow that divebombed my head. "Most," I allowed, clinging to the fact that I could still see the feathered furies, even if I couldn't interpret their presence. "But I can still see the ley lines, so I think I have enough."

"Enough for what?"

"To take you back with me."

Lucan tried again to object. "Milady—"

"It's the only way, Lucan," I said, with far more certainty than I felt in my jelly-like center. "Our priority is getting Elysabeth back to the others."

He came to me then, my not-protector and not-quite-friend. Came to me and stood shoulder to shoulder beside me, facing in the opposite direction so his back was to Kate, with Elysabeth at our feet. He pitched his voice low so that only I would hear what he said.

"You're tired," he said. "And by your own admission, every time you travel the ley, you lose more of your magick to it. More of yourself. What if you're wrong and you can't withstand it again? Or can't enter it at all? Once I leave here with Lady Elysabeth, once I'm back at the Earth house with her ..."

He trailed off, but I knew what he didn't want to say. His bond to the Earth Crone was complete now, and if she lived and I couldn't make the trip back on my own, he wouldn't be able to return for me, no matter how much he wanted to, because the magick that had created him had taken away his power to choose.

If I couldn't do this, I would be consigning myself—and Kate—to certain death. The latter cleared her throat, and I met her gaze in the faint glow from the flashlight now pointed at the floor.

"We need to make a decision here, guys," she said. "We don't have time to keep arguing. Lucan, you need to get Elysabeth back to the house. Claire, you're sure you can do this, right? I mean, you've done it before, so ..."

"I—" *I don't know,* I started to say, because it was only fair that she knew the truth, that she knew I couldn't guarantee her arrival back at the Earth house, let alone her survival. But before I could tell her, a black feathered body plummeted to the ground between us. Others followed. Dozens of them, until I stared at a cell floor covered in dead and dying crows.

And then, in a blaze of insight, I understood.

I remembered how the crows had burst from the woods as we stepped into the ley—and then followed us here. How Kate's skin had been cold against mine. How she'd made it seem necessary that she accompany us for Elysabeth's sake. How, when Lucan had kicked over the waste bucket a moment ago, she hadn't called on the goddess she was supposed to serve, but had instead said, *"Dear god."*

I raised my gaze from the dead crows to the person waiting for my response–the midwitch we had trusted—and then I saw it. The flicker in her eyes. The ugliness. How had I missed it? How could I not have known, not have sensed ...?

But there had been so much else. My son. Natalie. Braden. I'd been so grateful for Kate's help that I'd missed the truth buried beneath it, beneath the deceit. I'd missed that she hadn't asked why Lucan had said he would meet me in the garden, had only assured him that she would get me there—because she had already known we were going to the ley line. Because she'd planned it that way.

And I'd walked into the trap and brought Lucan with me.

It was on the tip of my tongue to shout a warning—to alert Lucan to the danger and let his instincts take over. To let him rip out the throat of—

Ice water washed through my gut. But what if the other was faster? What if it was Lucan who died, and not the other way around? What if Elysabeth never made it back to the others, and they lost their only chance to raise their collective magick?

Utter calm settled over me. I knew what I had to do.

I turned my gaze away from Kate before she could see what I had guessed. Before she turned on Lucan and Elysabeth. "She's right," I told the man at my side. "I can do this."

"But, milady—"

"Elysabeth is your priority," I reminded him. "Take her, and Kate and I will follow."

I looked up at him then and met the frustration in his eyes. The drive that surged in him and demanded that he save his Crone. His agony at knowing he had no choice.

I met all of it, and then I made myself smile because I *did* have a choice.

"We'll follow," I said again. "I can do this, Lucan. Trust me."

With a last, soft snarl of frustration, Lucan stooped and gently lifted his Crone from the cell floor. He cradled her against his chest, his arms forming a complete circle around her body.

She made no sound apart from the shallow rasp of her breath, but she wouldn't this time, because there was no Kate deliberately inflicting pain great enough to make an unconscious woman whimper.

My hands tightened around flashlight and staff. "Go," I urged.

And he did.

CHAPTER 28

I WAITED UNTIL THE LEY LINE'S SHIMMER SETTLED DOWN. Until its colors paled, and its undulations slowed, and I knew that Lucan was safely away with his precious cargo. Then I turned and shone the flashlight into the face of my one remaining companion.

"How long?" I asked. "How long have you been her?"

A torch flared to life on the wall behind me. Another a few feet away. Their pools of light danced out, overlapped, enveloped me. Me, and the being that was not Kate.

The brown eyes that were no longer hers met mine, a hint of surprise behind their coldness. "So, you figured it out, did you?" Morok asked, taking the flashlight from me with Kate's hand and tucking it into a pouch on her belt.

"How long?" I repeated. "You weren't her when I met her."

Morok laughed, and the dissonance of hearing it as Kate's laughter jarred me to the core. I curled my fingernails into my palms, clinging to the discomfort as my only anchor—the only reality I had left in a world I could no longer count on.

"I didn't even know she existed when you met her," he responded. "I didn't know *you* existed. My Mages were just after what they thought was one of the four pendants. You were quite the revelation to me, Claire Emerson."

He eyed me up and down as he strolled around me, tsking and shaking Kate's head, the touch of his gaze almost physical. My skin crawled under it.

"Seriously, I had no idea the Morrigan had that level of bait and switch in her," he mused. "All those centuries, she had me fooled. Almost outdid me at my own game. Almost." He stopped in front of me, and Kate's square, capable hand reached up to the silver chain around my neck. A single finger twisted around it and lifted it away from my skin, tugging at it, but the pendant remained beneath my shirt as if glued there. The chain bit into the back of my neck, and Morok's smile turned unpleasant.

"You might as well hand it over. You've lost."

It took everything in me not to knock the hand away. I stared at the flickering shadows cast by the torch on the cavern wall, refusing to react. Refusing to give him the satisfaction.

"*How long?*" I grated again from between my teeth. "And why?"

With a hiss of exasperation, Morok released the pendant's chain and dropped Kate's hand back to her side. "Not long after she helped save your family that night," he said, "when it became obvious that you would never grow into the power you'd been given. So much power, Lady Claire, and you just couldn't accept it, could you? Couldn't wield it the way Kate knew she would have done if the pendant had come to her instead of you."

He walked around me again, and I heard the crunch of fallen crows beneath Kate's boots.

"It made quite the impression on her when she held it that night, you know," he said. "She returned it to you so you could be who you were supposed to be, and she was *so* disappointed in you. So angry at how wasted it was on you. So certain she could do better. And now look. She's going to have it, just as I promised her she would."

"*She* will?"

"Semantics. Her. Me. Same thing now, right?" He shrugged. "As for why, I should have thought that obvious. She was my golden opportunity—my chance to be one of you."

One of—my blood turned to ice in my veins. Elysabeth's pendant—*that* was the plan? "You—Kate—"

Kate's voice chuckled again. Goddess, that was unnerving.

"Me," Morok agreed. "And Kate. We would have made an excellent addition to the Crones, don't you think? Skilled enough to take our place among the others, sympathetic enough to coax you out of what you so obviously never wanted. And we were so close—*so* close—to having the Earth pendant before you decided to try ley travel."

He looked over at the empty cot and shook Kate's head. "I hadn't expected that, I'll admit. Giving that bitch a new lease on life, then rounding up the others to come and save her. I had to adjust all kinds of plans because of you, Claire Emerson, but in the end ..." He reached out and patted my cheek with a Kate-hand. "In the end, it doesn't matter what pendant I hold. The outcome remains the same because the Crones will have no idea I'm among them until it's too late."

I thought I understood, but I needed to be sure, because deep in my brain, the tiny seeds of an idea were taking shape.

"So the battle at the house, the one we left ..."

"Oh, pshaw. That little tiff? It will already be over by the time I get back. The Mages will have crawled off with their tails between their legs, the Crones will be licking their wounds, the house will be repairing itself again—it's become very good at that, thanks to you—and I will arrive injured and broken and oh, so sad that you didn't make it with me." He sniffled and mimed wiping away a tear. "I'll be sure to tell them all about how very heroic you were, though, I promise. And then I'll reveal to them how the pendant chose me to replace you as Fifth Crone, and they'll accept me as one of their own, and they'll raise their magick, and I'll raise mine, and oh, but it will be beautiful. Spectacular, even. And then—"

"Elysabeth isn't even conscious, never mind capable of magick," I interrupted.

Morok grunted, and Kate's face frowned. "Yes. A small wrench in the works, I'll admit. But she'll recover, and it will be worth the wait, because *finally*, after all these centuries, I'll have my powers back—and I'll have used the Morrigan's own magick to open the portals. How delicious is that?"

Portals, plural?

Kate's brown eyes danced with amusement at the start of

surprise I couldn't hide. Her voice giggled, and Morok slapped a hand over her mouth and frowned. "*That* will take some getting used to," he mumbled behind it. Then he lowered the hand, and Kate's voice turned nasty. Vicious with Morok's words.

But not just Morok's words. Hers, too, because it was she who had opened the door to him in the first place. She who had invited him in, as Merlin had once done. She who had wanted the pendant and its power.

"You didn't really think I'd stop with just one portal, did you, Lady Claire?" they whispered. "Because I don't want back just a little of the power you bitches have stolen from me over the millennia. I want it all. Every last scrap you've taken from me. And when I have it, I will use it to crush your kind like the annoying, very *little* insects you are, and it will all be your fault. Yours alone, because you were too weak to claim what was given to you."

Kate's face thrust toward mine, so close that her spittle landed—icy cold—on my cheek as they hissed, "Now, give me the pendant!"

My grip shifted infinitesimally on the staff.

The seeds of my idea took root.

"The pendant, Crone!" Morok demanded.

"No."

Abruptly, Morok-Kate stepped back, and their voice softened. "He'll take it from you one way or the other, Claire. You know he will."

My heart skipped a beat. I peered into their face, searching for the woman behind the voice. The midwitch I'd once known. "Kate? You're still in there?"

For an instant, the brown eyes glimmered with sadness. With the real Kate. Then they closed over again, and she shook her head. "Give the pendant to him, and he'll make your death quick. If you make him wait, you'll die the way Elysabeth was dying—slowly and in agony. Your tongue will swell inside your mouth, your eyes will dry up like raisins, your brain will shrivel inside your skull, all your organs will shut down. Is that really how you want to go, Claire?"

I ignored the horror creeping across my skin and held out my hand to her in appeal. "Damn it, Kate, I know you're in there. Fight him!"

"I can't," Kate said. "And even if I could ..."

Morok returned to the brown eyes. "Even if she could," he finished, "she doesn't want to. There's no way out, Crone. The shifter cannot protect you. He will not come for you. No one will come for you. And I will still win."

The idea that had taken root unfurled and stretched out its branches. For a moment, I quailed from it, certain I had no chance of success.

"The pendant, Crone. *Now*."

I flinched from the harsh demand, and then I steeled myself. I had no other choice. I had to try. I raised my hand to the chain around my neck and lifted it over my head. The pendant resisted, refusing to leave the shelter of my shirt, pulling against me as if it knew my intentions.

No choice, I whispered to it in my mind.

It gave a final tug of objection, then let go and lifted from my chest. I held it aloft, letting it dangle and twirl at the end of its chain. Morok-Kate's eyes locked on it, gleaming with avarice. Triumph. Gloating.

"A wise decision," he said. "Now hand it over."

I tightened my sweaty grip on my staff, took a deep breath, and swung the pendant so that the chain wrapped around my fist—once, twice, three times.

"Come and get it," I retorted, and then I lunged toward the faint shimmer of the ley line into which Lucan and Elysabeth had disappeared.

The branches of my idea had contained many possibilities. I might have succeeded in getting to the ley with the pendant ahead of Morok—and then to the Earth house to warn the others about the imposter.

I might have succeeded in making it to the ley only to die within its magick—hopefully sending the pendant into the aether and forever out of his reach.

Or I might have succeeded in thrusting the pendant alone into the ribbon—again with the hope that it would disappear from his potential grasp.

I might have ... but I didn't.

As close as I was to the ley, and as fast as I bolted for it, Kate's body slammed into mine before I reached it. She knocked me, sprawling, onto the stone floor. Knocked the wind from my lungs. Knocked the pendant from a hold I'd thought to be like iron.

Instinctively, heedless of the filth into which I'd fallen, I rolled onto my back and swung my staff at her legs, knocking her feet out from under her. She grabbed for the pendant, but her hand fell short. Mine did not.

My fingers closed over the cold crystal in its ornate silver frame. Morok wrapped Kate's fingers in my hair and yanked me to my feet. He shook me so hard that my head snapped back and forth, and starbursts went off behind my eyes. Kate's hand wrapped around mine and pried at my fingers. I gritted my teeth and hung on for dear life.

My life.

My family's lives.

The life of the world itself.

We struggled and fell. Morok pulled me up again and threw me across the cell. My shin connected with the cot's metal frame, toppling me onto the thin, foul mattress. I hissed at the pain lancing through my leg, and Morok was on top of me, both of Kate's hands working at my grasp on the pendant. My fingers shook with the strain of holding on. Her nails clawed at my skin.

"Let go," my inner voice whispered.

"No," I moaned. "I can't—"

"Claire. Let go. Trust us."

Not one voice. A thousand of them. They came together in a murmur of sound, like the wind through trees. *"Let go, let go, let go ..."*

I hesitated. Morok wedged one of Kate's finger between mine and pried them away from the pendant. Reflexively, I tried to tighten my grip again.

The voices came together as one—calm, firm, certain. *"Let go."*

"All the witches that have gone before you," the memory of Edie's voice reminded me.

I gritted my teeth, squeezed my fist around the pendant as hard as I could one last time, and then—making the biggest leap of faith I had ever made in my entire life—pushed it and Morok-Kate away with all my strength.

My foe stood over me, wild-eyed and panting, looking as surprised as I felt at my sudden capitulation. But not as panicked.

I dug my fingers into the crusted mattress to keep from bolting up to seize the pendant back as a triumphant Morok draped it around Kate's neck. Then he turned on me, leaning down to grab my hair again and lift me half off the cot.

"Bitch!" he spat, Kate's brown eyes glittering with hatred. "I warned you, and now you will rot in here for eternity!"

He shook me ferociously, tossed me against the stone wall, and spun around. Without so much as a backward glance, he stalked across the cell, raising Kate's hand in a sweeping arc over her head. The torches flared high and bright, then extinguished.

Dark descended hard and fast, broken only by the faint ribbon of light that was the ley. I had no time to react. No time to push to my feet. No time to draw so much as a breath before Kate's silhouette merged with the glimmer and both disappeared.

The cell plunged into utter blackness. Utter silence. Seconds ticked past, an eternity between each of them as my random, disordered thoughts struggled to form.

I'd failed ... Morok was gone ... he'd left me to die—slowly, horribly, and alone—just as Kate had threatened, and he was going to win ... I was never going to see my family again ... or Keven ... or Lucan ... was that my staff in my hand, still? ... damn, but I'd forgotten how absolute the dark could be ... how in the world had I managed to keep hold of my staff?

Morok was going to win.

I pushed myself upright and sat on the cot's edge, flexing my cramped, staff-clutching fingers to ease their ache as I stared into the blackness that had so suddenly become my entire world. The idea of the dark god's victory played over and over in my head as I struggled to come to terms with it.

Morok had the pendant—*my* pendant. I had lost my last, desperate bid to keep it away from him, and now his victory was assured. Maybe not immediately, but eventually, because no one else knew. No one had any idea.

He would live among the Crones as one of them. He would help them to raise their power—the Morrigan's power. And then he would steal it from them, and centuries of sacrifice would be for nothing, and there wasn't a damned thing I could—

A brilliant light sliced through the dark before me, and I threw a hand up to shield my eyes. My heart leapt into my throat. Morok. He'd come back to finish—

My brain dismissed the idea before it finished forming. Morok had meant what he'd said about making me suffer. This had nothing to do with him. It was ... what?

I blinked away the spots dancing across my vision and lowered my hand back to my lap. The light's brilliance died down and became a bright, undulating glow. A ribbon. A ley? But how? I had no pendant. I had no magick. How could I possibly see—

My breath caught as a thousand faces shimmered to life within the ribbon's depths, each lined with the years and all that those years had contained for its owner. Each set with a courage and steadfastness that took away my breath. Each staring at me as I did at them, as if waiting for me to—

Slow realization unfurled in me, and my hand tightened on my staff.

The faces weren't *in* the ley, they *formed* the ley. But how—and where ...?

"*Come*," they whispered, and a single hand stretched out from the ribbon toward me.

I hesitated for all of a nanosecond before I rose and stepped forward—just long enough for my earlier sluggish thoughts to become rapid-fire.

Because it didn't matter where the ley led. It mattered only that I wouldn't die here. That I *would* see my family again. That I would have the chance to warn the others about the false Kate in their midst.

I gripped my staff firmly in one hand and reached for the ley-hand with my other.

And my favorite thought of all?

Like *fuck*, Morok was going to win.

The ley-hand closed around mine, and I dissolved.

The End

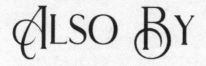

ALSO BY

The Crone Wars

Becoming Crones

A Gathering of Crones

Game of Crones

The Grigori Legacy

Sins of the Angels (Grigori Legacy book 1)

Sins of the Son (Grigori Legacy book 2)

Sins of the Lost (Grigori Legacy book 3)

Sins of the Warrior (Grigori Legacy book 4)

Other Books by Linda Poitevin

Gwynneth Ever After

Forever After

Forever Grace

Always and Forever

Abigail Always

Shadow of Doubt

ACKNOWLEDGEMENTS

I owe heartfelt thanks to the many people in my world who helped get this book into your hands, dear reader.

This time around, a big shout-out goes to my writing friend Marie Bilodeau, who provided clarity, support, and the best sounding-board ever when I ran into plot problems. I think I'd still be angsting over things if it hadn't been for her! And the way this book ends? You can blame that on her, too. ☺

Thanks go again to Luke Marty of Your Beta Reader for his feedback on the story and suggestions for improving it, and to Laura Paquet, for her fantastic-as-always copy edits and attention to detail. My words do what I meant them to do because of these people, and I am forever grateful for their help.

A special mention to Claude Cadieux, whose locating spell turned up some missing (and critical!) story notes that I thought I'd lost. Keep an eye out in the next book for that spell, which Claude has kindly said I can share with Claire—and with you!

And of course, my gratitude and love remain undiminished for my husband, my family, and the many women who are a part of my real-life gathering of Crones. None of this would be possible without their support (and return love), and I am so, so lucky to have them in my life.

About The Author

Lydia M. Hawke is a pseudonym used by me, Linda Poitevin, for my urban fantasy books. Together, we are the author of eleven books that range from supernatural suspense thrillers to contemporary romances and romantic suspense.

Originally from beautiful British Columbia, I moved to Canada's capital region of Ottawa-Gatineau more than thirty years ago with the love of my life. Which means I've been married most of my life now, and I've spent most of it here. Wow. Anyway, when I'm not plotting the world's downfall or next great love story, I'm also a wife, mom, grandma, friend, walker of a Giant Dog, keeper of many cats, and an avid gardener and food preserver. My next great ambition in life (other than writing the next book, of course) is to have an urban chicken coop. Yes, seriously…because chickens.

You can find me hanging out on Facebook at facebook.com/LindaPoitevin, and on my website at LydiaHawkeBooks.com, where you can also join my newsletter for updates on new books (and a free story!)

I love to hear from readers and can be reached at lydia@lydiahawkebooks.com. And yes, I answer all my emails!